A Lesson Learned

The Willowbrook Series
Book 4

By Laura Landon

Text by Laura Landon
Cover by Dar Albert

Dragonblade Publishing, Inc. is an imprint of Kathryn Le Veque Novels, Inc.
P.O. Box 23
Moreno Valley, CA 92556
ceo@dragonbladepublishing.com

Produced in the United States of America

First Edition October 2023
Trade Paperback Edition

ARE YOU SIGNED UP FOR DRAGONBLADE'S BLOG?

You'll get the latest news and information on exclusive giveaways, exclusive excerpts, coming releases, sales, free books, cover reveals and more.

Check out our complete list of authors, too!

No spam, no junk. That's a promise!

Sign Up Here

www.dragonbladepublishing.com

Dearest Reader;

Thank you for your support of a small press. At Dragonblade Publishing, we strive to bring you the highest quality Historical Romance from some of the best authors in the business. Without your support, there is no 'us', so we sincerely hope you adore these stories and find some new favorite authors along the way.

Happy Reading!

CEO, Dragonblade Publishing

Additional Dragonblade books by Author Laura Landon

The Willowbrook Series

A Willowbrook Miracle (Book 1)

A Page Turner Bookshop (Book 2)

A Bitter Pill to Swallow (Book 3)

A Lesson Learned (Book 4)

Men of Valor Series

A Love For All Time (Book 1)

A Love That Knows No Bounds (Book 2)

A Love That's Worth The Risk (Book 3)

A Love That Heals the Heart (Book 4)

Prologue

Spencer Washburn, Earl of Carnhaven, rode up the lane to Carnhaven Manor with an overwhelming sense of excitement. He'd only intended to be gone for a week at the most, but instead, he'd had to spend the last two weeks in London tending to business.

He couldn't wait to get home. Couldn't wait to see his wife and daughters. He'd missed them more than he ever imagined he would. He never thought he'd turn into such a family man. Never thought he'd become so domesticated.

"Welcome home, Lord Carnhaven," his butler Jasper greeted him, opening the door to let him enter.

"Greetings, Jasper. Is my wife here?"

"No, my lord. She took the girls down to the lake for a ride in the boat."

Spencer tipped his head back and laughed. "I swear Lady Carnhaven would live on the water if I'd let her. I'm terribly afraid she'd turn my daughters into fish if she could."

"Yes, my lord. I don't doubt she would. She does love the water, she does."

"Yes, she does. I think I'll go down to the lake and get her. Would you ask Cook to prepare an early luncheon? I haven't eaten yet today and am quite hungry."

"Of course, my lord. Cook will have something ready by the

time you return with her ladyship and your daughters."

"Thank you, Jasper," Spencer said, then raced out the door. He couldn't wait to see his wife and daughters. Couldn't wait to hold them. He'd thought of nothing else from the moment he left London.

He mounted his horse and galloped to the lake.

Caroline was already in the boat with the girls sitting near her when he caught sight of her. Five-year-old Cassandra sat toward the front, near the servant rowing the boat, and two-year-old Felicity clung to her mother's knee.

Spencer dismounted and leaned against a tree while he watched his family enjoying their lark. He could tell how much they relished this time on the water. His wife's head was tipped gently back so she could absorb every second of the sun as their little boat cut prettily through the still pond. His heart swelled as he took in the sight of his precious family in front of him.

At that moment, Caroline turned her attention to the riverbank and saw him. Her eyes lit with love, and she jumped to her feet. She lifted her arm in the air and waved with excitement.

The boat rocked, but she held steady.

"Sit down, Caroline," he called. "You'll fall."

"No, I won't," she said on a laugh.

"Yes, you will."

Spencer took a step toward the water.

Caroline teetered in the boat.

"Spencer!" she called out as she lost her balance.

"Sit down, Caroline!"

At that moment, though, she lost her balance and toppled over the side of the capsizing boat.

"Caroline!"

Spencer pulled off his boots and rushed into the water as the small rowboat tipped precariously and tossed the occupants into the water.

The servant rowing the boat came to the surface and reached for Cassandra. He brought her to shore, then went back in to save Mrs. Carnaghy, the nursemaid.

Spencer had already reached the boat but couldn't see Caroline anywhere. What he saw, though, was little Felicity gasping beneath the water.

His baby was drowning. She wasn't going to survive if he didn't save her.

Spencer reached for the struggling child and brought her to shore. He placed her on the grass and dove back in to search for Caroline but couldn't find her anywhere.

"Caroline! Caroline!"

Spencer searched for what seemed an eternity but couldn't find his wife anywhere. Finally, two Carnhaven servants heard the cries for help and ran to the pond's edge. They dove into the water and turned the small boat over. Caroline was trapped beneath it.

Spencer pulled her from the water and clutched her in his arms.

"Breathe, darling! Breathe!"

He took her to the bank of the river and nestled her close to him, as if his nearness would bring her back to life. But it didn't. There was no life left in her.

Spencer held her for several heart-wrenching moments, then turned to where Mrs. Carnaghy held his youngest daughter.

Felicity lay in the nursemaid's lap, playing with the woman's bonnet strings and laughing as if she'd just had a grand adventure.

Spencer's heart hardened. An agonizing pain stabbed through him, and he regretted the move he'd just made. He'd chosen to save his daughter at the cost of his wife. He'd saved Felicity instead of Caroline.

Caroline was dead and Felicity was alive.

He looked at his wife lying lifeless in his arms and realized he'd made the wrong decision. He should have saved Caroline.

He rose to his feet and carried Caroline in his arms back to Carnhaven Manor. Tears streamed down his cheeks and his heart tightened inside him.

Felicity was alive because he'd made the wrong choice. He'd never forgive his daughter for that.

CHAPTER ONE

EMMA SULLIVAN WALKED down the candlelit hallway in the Earl of Pearlman's townhouse and quietly opened the door to her charges' room. Both girls were sleeping soundly.

Emma stepped over to their beds and pulled the covers beneath their chins, then stopped when she reached the door and looked back on the two sisters. She'd grown increasingly fond of them over the past three years that she'd been their governess and dreaded thinking about the day she'd have to leave them. But that day was rapidly approaching. It wouldn't be long before their parents would send them to finishing school. Perhaps as early as next month.

Emma stepped back into the room and studied the two sleepy girls tucked in their beds. Pauline was the younger of the two and by far the prettiest. She had the enviable golden-blonde hair and sky-blue eyes that were all the rage. Emma had no doubt that when the girl made her come-out, she would be the belle of the ball and at the top of every eligible male's list as the most sought-after debutante. She would have more suitors than Lord and Lady Pearlman could contend with. Without a doubt, she would settle for nothing less than the title of duchess.

But Violet was the more intriguing of the two.

She was blessed with hair a luscious shade of auburn. When she stood in the sunlight, streaks of red colored the strands, making her soft curls appear a deep, dark red. But what set her apart from her sister was her keen mind and sharp wit.

Where Pauline was mostly interested in the latest fashion of the season, Violet was interested in the workings of anything mechanical or practices that allowed their estates to grow and prosper. If Emma could choose the perfect life for Violet, it would be helping a husband care for their land and run their estates.

If she could wish any life for the girl, it would be an active life with purpose. Otherwise, Violet would be bored with nothing to do. And she would have to find a husband who didn't care overly much for looks, because Violet wasn't blessed with the same stunning looks as Pauline.

Oh, not that she wasn't pretty. She was, in a fresh, sunny sort of way. But the thick glasses she was forced to wear detracted from her features. At least she could see moderately well—well enough not to run into things when she went without wearing her glasses, like her mother tried to insist she should do when in Society.

Perhaps, though, Emma would never be privileged to know what became of the girls. She'd overheard Carrie, their personal maid, say Lady Pearlman had already spoken to her about accompanying the girls when they left for finishing school. Emma wondered what she would do then. She definitely wouldn't stay here and be relegated to the position of an upstairs maid. Everyone knew what eventually happened to the upstairs maids when Viscount Slushman, the Earl and Countess of Pearlman's reprobate son, cornered them. They were summarily dismissed without a reference and with Slushman's babe growing in their belly.

Emma wasn't going to stay around until that happened to her. There were several options more appealing than that. She desperately wanted children of her own, but not any who were born with red hair and blue eyes who would remind her of Randall Slushman.

Emma turned away from the room and had taken only three

steps when she heard a muffled scream coming from further down the hall, close to her own room.

There was no doubt that the frightening scream had come from her best friend.

"Janey!" she called out, and raced toward the girl's room.

Young Slushman had Janey pinned against the wall and her gown ripped to her waist. Her breasts were bared and there were scratches reddening her flesh. But Janey had done her best to fight back and cause as much damage to Slushman as she could.

He already had several deep cuts down the side of his face from where Janey had raked her fingernails along his cheek. The reprobate howled in pain as streams of blood ran from the wounds and stained his white linen shirt.

"Damn you!" Slushman bellowed as he swiped his shirt sleeve across his cheek, then pulled back his arm and hit Janey with his fist.

Emma rushed into her own room and grabbed the nearest object she saw—a metal letter opener she'd used to open a box earlier in the day. She rushed back into Janey's room, lifted the letter opener, and jabbed it deep into Slushman's side with all her might. The blade ground against flesh, then struck bone. Emma pulled the letter opener from him and struck again.

Slushman bellowed a pain-filled cry, then clutched his hand to his side. Blood pulsed between his fingers as he glared at her with a venomous look.

Emma took a defensive step away from him and stumbled when he attempted to take another step. Before he reached her, however, his eyes rolled to the back of his head and he crumpled to the floor.

"Is he dead?" Janey cried, clutching her ripped gown to cover her breasts.

"I don't know," Emma whispered as she felt shock overtake her. She stared at the still figure lying on the floor. "We have to get out of here before his lordship returns. Change your gown and pack as much as you can get into a valise."

"Where are we going?" Janey asked.

"I don't know," Emma answered, pushing Janey into her room. She threw Janey's valise onto the bed and stuffed the only gown hanging on the door into the valise, then opened the drawers to her dresser and took out some nightclothes. When she looked back to Janey, her friend sat on the bed with her arms clutched around her trembling body and her teeth chattering.

"Are you all right?" Emma asked.

"Yes, but I'm afraid."

"I know," Emma said. "I'm scared, too." She pulled a cover from Janey's bed and wrapped it around her friend's shoulders. "Do you have any money?"

"In the bottom drawer."

Janey pointed to the drawer, and Emma opened it and removed a threadbare clutch purse. It only contained a few coins.

"It's not much."

"It will help," Emma said, then rushed to her room and threw her few clothes into a bag. She buried the little money she'd managed to save since she'd taken the position of governess to the two Slushman girls in a coin purse at the bottom of her valise. With the coins that Janey had, they'd be able to ride the mail coach at least a few miles from London.

Emma closed her valise and wrapped a cloak around her shoulders, then ran to Janey's room to get her. She stopped short when she entered the room.

Janey was barely conscious as she sat on the bed. Blood soaked through her gown, and the bruises Slushman had given her had already turned dark.

"Let's go, Janey. We have to leave."

"You go without me, Emma. I'll only slow you down."

"I'm not leaving you. Now, come on."

Janey stood slowly and clutched at her damaged gown as she took a step toward the door.

"Wait!" Emma was desperate for them to escape, but she couldn't take the poor girl on a train or coach in her condition.

Emma retrieved the gown she had packed in Janey's satchel. As swiftly as she could, she got the girl changed into the fresh gown and stuffed the damaged one into the satchel. There would be plenty of time later to restore it to some semblance of respectability.

"There now," she said, trying hard to sound calm. "Good as new."

Emma wrapped her arm around Janey and almost had to carry her down the stairs. She was never so relieved as when they reached the outdoors.

Before they'd gone very far, a delivery driver stopped to give them a lift in the back of his wagon. Miraculously, they made their way to the mail coach before anyone saw them.

Emma paid for two tickets, then helped Janey into the coach and climbed in beside her. Thankfully, there was only one other passenger. He had obviously spent a hard night drinking and had passed out in the corner of the coach.

"How are you?" Emma asked.

"I'll feel better when we're out of London," Janey replied.

"Me too." Emma looked out the window. "Here comes the driver. We're going to leave now."

"Good," Janey said on a sigh.

The mail coach shifted when the driver climbed aboard, and Janey and Emma jerked in their seats as the horses lurched forward.

Emma pulled a carriage blanket across her friend's lap once they were on their way. "You rest now. We'll be traveling about four hours northwest of here. To some new little town called Willowbrook."

Janey made a soft noise that sounded like approval.

"What? Do you know someone in Willowbrook?"

"I might," she answered. "I'm just not sure he knows me anymore. Or wants to."

Janey turned her head away from Emma and closed her eyes. There was obviously a story here that Janey wasn't comfortable sharing. Emma didn't blame her. Everyone had secrets they would rather keep to themselves. Even Emma had secrets she hoped no one ever discovered.

She settled back against the poorly cushioned seat and closed her eyes. She prayed she would fall asleep but couldn't. Randall Slushman's body appeared before her. Blood oozed from the stab wounds she'd caused with the letter opener and turned his gleaming white shirt a bloody black.

Emma made sure Janey was comfortable, then shifted her friend's head to rest on her shoulder. Janey wasn't sleeping. Tears streamed down her face and her shoulders shook as she sobbed.

"What is going to happen to us, Emma?"

Emma reached for Janey's hand and held it. "I don't know, but as long as we're together, we'll be fine."

Janey tightened her grip on Emma's fingers, and after a long while, they both fell asleep.

"WAKE UP, JANEY. We're here."

Janey sat up with a start. "Is this Willowbrook?"

"Yes. This must be the main street. Nearly all the buildings have businesses in them."

"Willowbrook is larger than I thought it would be," Janey said, checking out the signs on the windows. "They have a bookstore. The Page Turner Bookshop."

"And a doctor. There's his clinic. Do you need to see a doctor?"

"No, I'm fine."

"I'm not sure you are," Emma said, but wasn't sure either of them were up to answering the questions a doctor would ask when he saw Janey's injuries. "The sun has barely risen," Emma remarked. "Willowbrook is just starting to wake. Do you want to walk for a bit before the streets get crowded?"

When Janey didn't answer, Emma turned to see what had captured her friend's attention. Janey stood in the center of the walk and stared at a man just stepping from his carriage.

The man wasn't overly tall, perhaps just shy of six feet, but his shoulders were broad and his arms muscular, as if he spent a great deal of time outdoors chopping wood. He wore a hat and cloak, and before he reached the door of the establishment, he took keys from his pocket. He turned before he inserted his key into the lock, as if checking his surroundings, and his gaze locked with Janey's.

A look of disbelief stole the color from his face, and the keys that opened the door to ISAAC REYNOLDS – SOLICITOR AT LARGE fell to the ground.

"Janey?"

"Isaac."

Tears ran down Janey's cheeks, and she seemed frozen in place as the handsome man who'd called her by name took several steps toward her. When he reached her, he wrapped his arms around her and brought her close to him in a warm embrace.

"What are you doing here?" he asked, cupping her cheeks in the palms of his hands and taking note of the marks and bruises. "What happened to you?" he said, frowning at the scratches on her face and neck. "Never mind." He turned her toward his office door. "Let me get you inside." He scooped up the keys that had fallen to the ground and put them in the lock. When the door opened, he led her inside.

Emma followed them and closed the door behind her.

"Come with me," he said, taking Janey's hand and leading them through his office and into a private room with a table and several chairs in the center. "Please, sit down. I'll make tea."

"That would be appreciated," Emma said.

"My name is Isaac Reynolds," he said while he put a kettle of water on a small potbellied stove and stoked it with a shovelful of coal. "Janey and I have been acquainted since we were young."

"Perhaps *more* than just acquainted," Emma said, taking the cups and saucers from his hands.

"Yes, perhaps." He reached for Janey's hand and held it.

"Let me introduce you, Isaac," Janey said. "This is Emma Sullivan. She saved me."

He gave Emma a nod of greeting then turned back to Janey. "Saved you from what?"

Janey took a shaky breath before she spoke. "Emma and I have worked together for several years. For the Earl and Countess of Pearlman in London."

"I've heard of them," Isaac said. "Actually, I haven't heard as much about them as I've heard about their son."

"If what you heard was bad," Emma said, "then it was true."

"Emma was governess to their two daughters," Janey continued, "and I was an upstairs maid. Last night I… I was…"

Her fingers tightened around Emma's hand, and Emma continued for her. "Last night, Randall—Lord Slushman—cornered Janey in a darkened hallway and attempted to rape her."

Isaac's expression turned livid with rage.

"He tore her gown and caused the scratches and wounds you see. I heard her scream for help and came as fast as I could."

"Thankfully, Emma got there before Slushman could do me any real harm," Janey said.

"I stabbed him with a letter opener," Emma said. "Twice. I think I might have…" She clutched her hands and lowered her gaze to her fists. "I'm afraid I may have killed him."

"Do you know for sure?" Isaac asked.

"No, but he was losing a lot of blood when we left."

The kind fellow reached for Janey's hand and held it. "What are your plans now?"

Janey looked at Emma, and they both shrugged. "We don't really have any," Emma said.

"What brought you to Willowbrook?"

"Luck," Emma answered. "This was as far as the money we had between us would carry us."

Isaac grinned. "Then I'm extremely fortunate that you made it this far."

"You don't have to worry about us, Isaac," Janey said. "I'm not your responsibility."

A serious expression covered Isaac's face. "Are you anyone else's responsibility? Is there anyone else in your life?"

"No," Janey whispered. "There was never anyone in my life after you."

"I felt the same, Janey," he replied.

Isaac wrapped his arms around Janey and brought her close to him.

"Are you sure you're all right?" he asked when she winced.

"I'll be fine. I'm just a little sore."

"Come with me," he said, reaching for her hand.

"Where are we going?"

"To my home."

Janey pulled her hand from his grasp. "We can't."

"Why can't we?"

"What if someone sees us?"

"What if they do? You brought a chaperone with you."

Janey looked at Emma and smiled. "I suppose it will seem as if I did."

"Come on, sweetheart," Isaac said, and led them from his office to the carriage that was still waiting for him.

Emma and Janey stepped into the carriage first, followed by Isaac. The solicitor knocked on the carriage roof, making Janey wince as the carriage jolted forward.

"Are you sure you don't want to see a doctor?" he asked.

"Quite sure. The last thing I want is to draw attention to myself or to Emma."

"Very well," Isaac responded. "Then I'll take you home and get you into a warm bath and let Emma take care of you."

"That sounds perfect." Janey leaned her head back and closed her eyes. She was quiet for a short while before she spoke. "Why didn't you come to London when your brother died and you acquired the Wistrom title?"

The question shocked Emma. "You are the Earl of Wistrom?" she asked.

"I am," Isaac replied. "In name only. My father evicted me when I chose to become a solicitor. My older brother Franklin was the Wistrom heir and was left to take over when father died. My younger brother, Connor, was left to manage the estates if anything happened to Franklin. I was consigned to a life in the clergy."

"Which you did not relish."

"Which I could not tolerate," he said with bitterness in his voice.

Janey smothered a laugh, "You would have made a terrible vicar, Isaac."

"I would have made a very good vicar, I'll have you know—if that's what I had wanted to be."

"But it was not," Janey answered for him.

"No, it was not. I'm very content being what I am and living where I do. I do not miss the city and would never consider going back."

The carriage slowed, then turned into a shaded lane. It stopped in front of a stately mansion. Emma and Janey alighted, then looked up at the elegant Gothic Revival country house.

"Welcome to Ten Oaks," Isaac said with a smile on his face and pride in his voice.

"Oh, Isaac," Janey whispered. "Your home is magnificent."

"I'm glad you think so," he replied.

"I see why it's called Ten Oaks," Emma said, counting the massive oak trees lining either side of the lane.

"Yes. My mother was partial to oak trees and had them planted when she first saw the estate. It's been known as Ten Oaks ever since."

"They are beautiful," Janey said, but both Emma and Isaac cast looks in her direction when her voice sounded so weak. At just that moment, she seemed to lose her balance and staggered to the side.

"Janey," Isaac called out as he reached for her. "Come with me. Let me get you inside."

He took Janey into the house and escorted her to a room. "I'll let you take care of her, Emma. Mrs. Marble will help you, and I'll go alert the groundsman to report anything unusual."

"Thank you," Emma said, then draped a light cover across Janey, who had collapsed onto the bed. She was already asleep.

Emma sat beside the bed and reached for Janey's hand. They'd both gone through a lot since yesterday, but they couldn't give up yet. There was too much to go through before they were safe. Especially if Lord Slushman was dead. Especially if she'd committed murder.

Chapter Two

Spencer Washburn, Earl of Carnhaven, clutched his daughter Cassandra's small hand in his much larger one and walked with her down a street in the fast-growing town of Willowbrook. It had already been five years since he'd lost the love of his life, and, try as he might to forget that fateful day, he couldn't. He could only dull the memory of losing Caroline.

"Are we going to stop to see Mr. Reynolds?" Cassandra asked.

"I thought we might before we return home."

"But we need to stop at the bookshop, too, Papa. I promised Felicity I'd get her a new Tommy Turtle book."

"You know your sister cannot read," Spencer argued. "She's only seven years old."

"But she'll be eight in a couple of months, and she reads quite well, Papa. The familiar words, anyway."

"Who taught her to read?"

"No one, Papa. She learned by herself. And when she comes upon a word she doesn't know, she asks me."

"Why didn't you tell me this?"

"Because you never talk about Felicity, or ask anything about her."

Spencer didn't respond to his older daughter. Even though she was only ten and a half years old herself, she understood far more than a child that age was supposed to understand.

"Why don't you like Felicity as much as you like me?" she asked.

Spencer couldn't help but be shocked by the question. "I like both of you equally," he answered.

"No, you don't, Papa. Even Felicity knows you don't."

"That's not true, Cassandra."

"Is it because Felicity looks just like Mama and seeing her makes you feel sad?"

"You need to stop such talk. You don't know what you're saying. Now, where would you like to go first?"

"I think the milliner's. They have the best selection of ribbons, and Felicity needs a new ribbon for her purple bonnet."

"I don't remember seeing Felicity wear a purple bonnet."

"That's because she's never worn it in front of you."

Spencer stopped and looked down at his daughter. "Why is that?"

"Because the first time she wore her purple bonnet, Mrs. Randall told her that it made her look just like Mama."

Spencer studied Cassie's shy look as she stared down to the ground. How dare Mrs. Randall say something to remind them of Caroline? How dare she confirm what everyone in Willowbrook knew—that Felicity was the picture of her dead mother, from her golden hair and rosy cheeks to her midnight-blue eyes and upturned nose?

How dare everyone remind him of the woman he'd loved and lost so tragically?

"Where do you want to go next?" he asked.

"I think the cigar and tobacco shop."

Spencer tried to make a joke about her statement. "Have you decided to take up smoking?"

"Of course not, Papa. I want to buy you some tobacco for your pipe. Lord Fransman was smoking something last week when you invited him to call on you. It smelled exceptionally pleasant, and I thought Felicity and I wouldn't mind smelling that odor in the house."

"Oh, I see. Then we must be sure to get some. After that, where would you like to go next?"

"The bookshop. Then I think I'm done shopping."

"Good. By then I think you will have spent all my money."

"Oh, no I won't, Papa. Everyone knows you are one of the richest men in Willowbrook."

"They do?"

"Of course they do. Everyone knows you own a mine loaded with diamonds and rubies and emeralds and pearls. And that's not even counting the gold."

Spencer couldn't contain his laughter. He owned a coal mine that hadn't brought forth a diamond or ruby or emerald in its lifetime. And pearls? How exactly was he going to explain oysters to a child who had never seen the ocean?

"Remind me to sit you down some day and have a talk with you about what I own."

"Can Felicity sit with us? She says she likes to listen to you explain things."

"*May* Felicity sit with us. And yes, of course," Spencer said, then slowed when they reached the milliner's shop. "We're here," he said. "Don't spend all day in here or Mr. Reynolds will call it a day and go home before we reach his office."

"I won't," Cassie said, then entered the milliner's and purchased a purple ribbon in record time. After that they went to the tobacco shop and purchased several different choices of tobacco. Lastly, they stopped at the bookshop and purchased several books, mostly for Felicity, but one or two of them for Cassie, though she said she intended to let her sister read them as well.

When they finished, they walked down the street to Isaac Reynolds' solicitor's office. When they opened the door, the bell above the entrance rang twice, just as it always did when Cassie jiggled the door to announce their arrival.

"Well, if it isn't my favorite visitor," Isaac greeted her when they entered his office. "Did you lose your sister?"

"No," Cassie answered. "She didn't wish to come with us

today. She decided to stay home."

"Well, you tell her I'm really disappointed. I would have enjoyed seeing her."

"I'll tell her."

"Now, Cassie. Why don't you run into my special room and greet Mrs. Black? She'll be disappointed if she doesn't get to chat with you. Her cat just had kittens, and she tells me they are as cute as they can be."

"Oh," Cassie squealed, rushing to the room Isaac used for meeting with his clients.

"I got your note," Spencer said when they were alone. "You wanted to see me?"

"I do," Isaac said, pouring two glasses of whiskey and giving one of them to Spencer.

"Is something wrong?"

"The opposite, Spence."

"What is it? You look…happy."

"I am. I've met someone. Her name is Janey. I intend to ask her to marry me."

Spencer smiled. He'd been waiting for Isaac to meet the perfect woman and find the love that he'd found with Caroline.

"Congratulations!" he said, lifting his glass in a toast. "Where did you meet her?"

"Actually, I've known her for several years."

"And you just got around to asking her to marry you?"

"To be honest, I haven't asked her yet."

"You haven't? Why? You can't be afraid she'll turn you down."

"That's exactly what I'm afraid of," Isaac replied.

"I can't believe this. What kind of woman would refuse your proposal?"

"The kind of woman who believes marrying me would ruin my future."

"Why would she think that?" Spencer asked.

"Because I asked her to marry me several years ago, and my

father convinced her that if she married me he would disown me and ruin my life."

"So she left you?"

"Yes. I searched all over London for her but couldn't find her. So I left London and came here and set up my business."

"And you found her again?"

"Actually, she found me," Isaac said. "She and her friend left London and used all the money they had to purchase tickets on the mail coach. They only had enough to get as far as Willowbrook. I recognized Janey when she stepped off the coach, and I gave her sanctuary when I realized she had no place else to go." He lifted the decanter and refilled their glasses. "I'd like you to meet them, Spence."

"I'd be honored."

"Would you come to dinner tonight?"

"I'd love to," Spencer said, trying to disguise a twinge of sadness, because his best friend was finding true happiness, while he would never know such a thing again. "I shall look forward to meeting her. And her friend."

"I think you'll be impressed, Spence. Janey's friend is a force to be reckoned with. She was a governess in London. Janey tells me she was widely sought after for her abilities."

"I'm intrigued," Spencer said.

The two men chatted until Cassie came back from having tea with Mrs. Black. After they bade Isaac farewell, they walked back to Carnhaven.

Cassie held her father's hand and swung their clutched fingers back and forth. "May I ask you a question, Papa?"

"Of course, Cassie. What would you like to know?"

"How long would it take Felicity or me to walk to Grandmama's manor house?"

Spencer stopped short and looked down on his eldest daughter. "Walk? You cannot think to walk to your grandmama's."

"Whyever not?"

"Because you would be waylaid by robbers and footpads

before you got to the end of the lane. Besides, you would be eaten by wild beasts before you traveled halfway to your grandmama's."

"Oh," his daughter sighed thoughtfully, though not in the least fearfully. She was well accustomed to her father's exaggerations.

"Whyever would you think you wanted to walk to your grandmother's?"

"It wasn't my idea. It was Felicity's."

"Well, whatever made her think that I would allow her to walk to her grandmother's?"

"She said you would never miss her, that you wouldn't even realize she was gone."

"That's not true," Spencer argued vehemently.

"Yes, it is, Papa. Are you sure she's at home now? Are you sure she hasn't already left?"

Spencer's blood turned to ice, and he grabbed Cassie's hand and pulled her along behind him.

"Don't worry, Papa," she said as she tried to keep up with him. "She's home. She wasn't going to leave yet."

Spencer stopped to catch his breath. "Are you sure?"

"Yes, I'm sure."

"Don't scare me like that, Cassie."

She looked up at him and smiled. "I told Felicity you'd care if she left us."

"Of course I'd care!"

Spencer took his daughter's hand and continued the rest of the way home at a faster pace. The minute they entered the house, he handed his packages to a waiting footman and climbed the stairs. He made his way to Felicity's room and opened the door.

His daughter sat at her desk reading a book. He didn't know what the book was called, but it was a much larger one than she should have been able to read.

Spencer wondered how much more there was about his youngest daughter that he didn't know.

CHAPTER THREE

EMMA DRESSED FIRST, then went to Janey's room to help her get ready for their guest's arrival. Their dinner guest was the Earl of Carnhaven, Isaac's best friend. Emma knew Isaac had invited him to dinner to meet Janey and gain his approval.

She hoped he approved. If the pompous earl found one thing wrong with Janey, she was prepared to defend her friend with every ounce of her ability. She was ready to go to battle on Janey's behalf if their guest uttered one disparaging remark.

"There," Emma said, looking in the mirror to assess Janey's hair. "You are a vision." When the housekeeper had appeared late that afternoon with a robin's-egg-blue satin dinner gown, Emma had known all eyes would be on Janey. The mirror only confirmed her earlier suspicions.

"Let's hope our guest thinks so."

"Our guest's opinion doesn't matter. The only opinion that counts is that of Isaac Reynolds. And he is already smitten with you."

"And," Janey said shyly, "I am smitten with him."

"You'd be a fool if you weren't."

"He is rather perfect, isn't he, Emma?"

"Yes, rather." Emma smiled. "Now, are you ready to go down?"

"Yes," Janey answered, and walked to the door. They descended the stairs together, and Emma paused behind Janey when Isaac stood at the bottom step and held out his hand.

"My love," he said. "You are a picture of loveliness."

"You clean up quite nicely yourself," Janey teased.

Isaac reared his head back and laughed. "Come, my ladies. Let's go in and meet our guest."

He extended both arms so Emma and Janey could each take one and be escorted into the drawing room. When they crossed the threshold, Emma dropped his arm and took a step back so that Janey was front and center for her introduction.

"Spencer, Lord Carnhaven, allow me to present Miss Janey Franklin."

"Miss Franklin," Lord Carnhaven said with a regal bow. "You are the picture of perfection."

"Lord Carnhaven," Janey said, performing a perfect curtsy. "It is a pleasure to meet you."

"Likewise," Carnhaven answered.

"And this is Miss Emma Sullivan," Isaac said.

"Miss… Sullivan," Lord Carnhaven said, pausing as he studied Emma.

"Lord Carnhaven," Emma said, executing a curtsy.

"It is a pleasure to meet you, Miss Sullivan."

"Likewise, my lord."

"May I offer you ladies a glass of wine?" Isaac asked.

"That would be lovely," Emma and Janey said in unison.

Isaac filled two glasses with a sweet red wine and gave one to each of them.

Emma was glad she had a glass of wine to hold in her hands. It gave her something to concentrate on other than the unbelievably handsome man sitting across from her. She'd met several attractive men in her line of work, but never had she been in such close social proximity to someone as perfectly proportioned as the Earl of Carnhaven.

His hair was a rich walnut and a little longer than most of the nobility wore. It curled at the ends most invitingly, causing

Emma's fingers to flutter of their own accord.

And his complexion was the most appealing bronze. It made his deep midnight-blue eyes seem to leap out and grab her attention. She'd never met anyone quite so mesmerizing.

"So," Lord Carnhaven said, breaking the silence that she'd absently allowed to linger. "Isaac tells me that you and Miss Franklin are recently from London."

"Yes, we worked together for several years and dreamed of leaving the city and residing in the country. We saved our money until we had acquired enough to get us this far."

"Which was a blessing indeed for Isaac," he said, casting a glance to where Isaac and Janey sat together on the sofa. The two were so engrossed in each other that they hardly realized Emma and Lord Carnhaven were in the room. "They seem quite fond of each other," he added with a smile.

"They are more than fond of each other," Emma countered. "They're in love."

"Of course they are," Carnhaven agreed. "Miss Franklin is all Isaac has talked about since the two of you arrived. All that's left is for Isaac to ask Miss Franklin to marry him." He paused and focused on Emma.

"What?" she asked.

"Will she accept his proposal, do you think?"

"That will be her decision to make."

"But you think she may not?" he asked in disbelief.

"I don't know. I'm not privy to her thoughts."

"I think you more than anyone else would know her thoughts, Miss Sullivan."

"I want nothing more than for Janey to be happy. If marriage to Isaac will bring about that end, then that is what I want for her."

"And what about you, Miss Sullivan?"

"Me?" Lord Carnhaven's question took her aback. "What about me?"

"Are you searching for a man to marry?"

"No, my lord. I have no interest in marriage. Not now. Not ever."

From the expression of shock and disbelief on his face, Emma presumed her answer surprised him.

"You have no intention of marrying and having children of your own?"

"Do you find that so difficult to believe, my lord?"

"I do, Miss Sullivan. Especially for a woman whose life's work is to educate and rear other parents' children to be model adults. One would think you would take the greatest pleasure in showering your own children with those same advantages."

Emma had always dreamed of having children of her own, until that night when her dream had been shattered and she realized no man would ever want her as the mother of his children. Now, she was not only a woman no man would want to marry—she was probably a woman who had committed murder.

"Some women are best nurturing children who are not their own rather than marrying and having children."

Emma was saved from having to respond further to Lord Carnhaven when the butler rapped on the door and announced that dinner was served.

Isaac rose and escorted Janey in to dinner, and Lord Carnhaven rose to escort Emma. At first she hesitated to take the earl's hand, but soon realized it would seem oddly impolite to refuse. Besides, what possible reason could there be to refuse? It wasn't that she had been totally ruined, by any means. She had simply been disgraced and branded a pariah by her family and the rest of Society. That was the moment she realized she would never have the life she'd been raised to believe would be hers. That she could not *expect* that kind of life to be hers.

Emma placed her hand in the earl's and rose to her feet. For the first time since that fateful night, she felt a plethora of emotions she'd never felt before. Emotions that engulfed her body and caused a smoldering fire to burn inside her.

She fought the waves of heat she'd never experienced before.

"Is something wrong?" Lord Carnhaven asked as they followed Isaac and Janey into the dining room.

"Of course not," she answered, desperate to separate her hand from where it rested on his sleeve but knowing she could not without drawing undue attention to herself.

Lord Carnhaven seated her at the table and sat beside her. A footman filled their glasses with wine, and Emma lifted the glass to her mouth. She drank a small bit, then placed her glass on the table and looked at him. He was watching her.

Emma knew it was essential that she carry on a conversation with him. He would think she was intimidated by him if she did not, and that was the last impression she wanted to give him, even if it was partially true.

"Isaac tells us that you have two daughters. What are the ages of your girls?"

"Cassandra is almost eleven and Felicity is almost eight."

"Ah, the perfect ages to explore and discover the world around them. What are their interests?"

He thought for a moment, a frown on his forehead.

"Are you unsure of your daughters' likes and dislikes?"

With a hint of frustration in his expression, the Earl of Carnhaven showed Emma a flash of irritation. "No, of course not. I just find their likes and dislikes difficult to explain."

"And do you find that unusual?" she asked.

"What? That a parent finds it difficult to understand his children?"

"No," Emma countered. "Not that a father finds it difficult to understand his daughters."

"Then what?"

Emma took in a deep breath of air and slowly released it. She wasn't sure how much she had a right to say, and yet something told her the Earl of Carnhaven was at a loss to understand his daughters. As time went on, instead of growing closer to his daughters, they would all grow further apart.

"Emma," Janey said from across the table. "Whatever are you

and Lord Carnhaven discussing? You both look as if you are planning a battle maneuver."

Emma forced a smile to brighten her face. "Not anything near as dramatic as that, Janey. Just planning our strategy for defeating you and Isaac in an after-dinner game of whist."

"You think you can defeat us at a game of whist?" Isaac said.

Emma turned to lock her gaze with Lord Carnhaven's. "The earl assures me he is an excellent card player."

"Does he now?" Isaac teased.

"He does. He assured me several times during our discussion that he is quite proficient at not only cards, but several other challenging games."

Emma made the mistake of shifting her focus to Lord Carnhaven. If looks could burn a hole through skin, she would be in need of the salve Cook kept on hand for kitchen burns.

"Well," Isaac said, lifting his wine glass to make a toast. "I will instruct the staff to serve dessert after the winners are declared. Until then, may the best team win."

When the toast was finished, Lord Carnhaven assisted Emma to her feet. "I don't mind coming out the loser," she whispered in an effort to make him feel more at ease.

"I do. I never accept losing—at anything," he replied as they marched into the drawing room.

"WHY DIDN'T I know that you were such an outstanding card player?" Isaac said before taking another swallow of his wine.

This must have been Isaac's third or perhaps fourth glass since Spencer and Emma trounced him and Janey.

"Because you have never invited me to play cards with you."

"And now I know why," Isaac said. He lowered his glass and leveled on Spencer a mockingly serious glare. "How are you at chess?"

Spencer couldn't stop a smile from lifting his lips. "Chess would be my game of choice, were I ever to be asked."

"I don't believe this."

"Believe it, my friend. I'm a master at many things."

"Is there anything at which you are not a master?" Emma said when she and Janey entered after a visit to the retiring room.

Spencer gave her a challenging look. "I'm not sure, Miss Sullivan. But if I have overlooked something, I'm sure you will point it out."

"Be assured that I will," the lady said, and Spencer couldn't help but smile. He wasn't certain if it was all the wine he'd had, or the looks of admiration she gave him when he made an outstanding play at whist. Or perhaps it was the hint of a wink that preceded her smile. Whatever it was, he found that although she irritated him more often than not, she impressed him at the same time.

He didn't want to admit that she intrigued him, but she did, even though he'd sworn no woman would ever interest him again. His wife still held a special grip on his heart. She was the other half of his soul, and no one would ever take her place. Especially a woman who was as strong-willed and opinionated as Emma Sullivan.

Spencer vowed he would never spend another moment thinking about Miss Sullivan. He didn't need the kind of trouble she would bring with her.

And trouble *would* follow her—in spades.

CHAPTER FOUR

JANEY WAS GOING to marry Isaac Randolph.

Isaac had asked her a few days after their dinner party with Lord Carnhaven, and after thinking on it overnight, and a long discussion with Emma, she accepted.

Emma had never seen two people happier than Janey and Isaac. They spent every moment together making plans for their nuptials. The banns had already been read once in church, to loud applause from the congregation. Of course, no one objected. Everyone was overjoyed at the good news. Even the row of elderly spinsters smiled and nodded their approval.

Emma held a small open house to introduce Janey to the list of friends Isaac had invited. It wasn't a large gathering, just a few of Isaac's friends and neighbors. Of course, Lord Carnhaven was at the top of the list, along with his two daughters, Cassandra and Felicity. Emma was exceedingly pleased to finally meet them.

"Miss Sullivan," Carnhaven said, bringing his daughters to her. "Please, allow me to introduce my daughters. This is Lady Cassandra, and this is Miss Felicity."

Both girls executed perfect curtsies. "Miss Sullivan," they said in unison.

"It's a pleasure to meet you, Lady Cassandra. Miss Felicity."

"Father tells us you are a close friend of Miss Franklin's," Cassandra said.

"I am," Emma responded. "And Mr. Randolph tells me you are both special friends of his."

The two girls exchanged smiles. "We are," they said in unison.

"Well, do you know what *that* means?" Emma said as if she had a great secret.

"I do," Felicity answered.

"I don't," Cassandra admitted. "What does it mean?"

"It means that we are destined to be great friends, too."

"Oh!" Lady Cassandra said with growing excitement. "Of course."

"So, have you young ladies had a piece of that chocolate cake yet?"

"Not yet," Cassandra said. "Papa said it's impolite to eat before everyone else has."

"Of course, your Papa is correct, but I've been watching, and I think everyone has already eaten, so you may have a piece of cake now. Come with me and I'll escort you to the refreshment table."

Emma led the way, and the Earl of Carnhaven's daughters followed her. When they reached the refreshment table, she made sure they each received a piece of chocolate and white marbled cake with butter frosting and a glass of lemonade. Then she found them seats at one of the tables and helped them settle. She turned around to check with Janey in case there was anything she could help her with, but before she took her first step, she collided with a solid wall of muscle.

"Thank you, Miss Sullivan," Lord Carnhaven said, clasping his fingers firmly around her upper arms to keep her from toppling over. "I appreciate your assistance with my girls. I should have been keeping better watch over them."

"That's quite all right, Lord Carnhaven. They're lovely. You should be very proud of them."

"I am," he said, looking over her shoulder to cast a glance at the pair as they giggled at something one of them said. He smiled as he turned his attention back to her. "Would you care to sit for a moment?"

Emma thought for a second. "Yes, I believe I would. I've been on my feet quite a long time today."

The earl escorted her to two chairs set off to the side. "Would you care for a lemonade, or something stronger?"

"A lemonade, please," she answered, and he left to get two glasses of lemonade. He handed her one when he returned.

"Would you mind if I asked your opinion on something?" he said before taking a long swallow of his lemonade.

"Of course not," she answered. "As long as it isn't personal. I don't care to talk about my personal life."

"No, it's nothing personal. It's about my daughters."

"Then I don't mind at all, except you must remember that I just met them. It's not as if I know them well."

"No, I'd just like your first impression of them."

Emma smiled. "Then what would you like to know?"

Lord Carnhaven took another sip of his lemonade. "How would you compare them? Other than in looks, are they more similar or different?"

"Oh, my lord. I find them far more different. Even though Felicity tells me she is not quite eight years old, it seems that she is the older sister, more observant and decisive. Cassandra appears to be the more outgoing of the two, where Felicity is far more inclined to stay in the background so as not to draw attention."

"You gathered all of that from just meeting them?" he said with a look of surprise.

Emma smiled. "People fascinate me, my lord. I just naturally notice things others might overlook at first glance." She finished her lemonade and placed her empty glass on a nearby table. "When meeting a new family by whom I've been hired, it's often essential to form opinions of my charges on the spur of the moment in order to get off on the right footing."

"Yes, I can see where that would be important," he said

thoughtfully. "So, what other first impressions have you formed concerning my daughters?"

Emma looked around her to make sure no one could overhear their conversation. "This is just an opinion based on a first meeting, my lord."

"I understand. But that is what I asked for."

"Very well." Emma took a deep breath and released it. "Your oldest daughter feels very comfortable around you, much loved. Much understood and accepted. Your younger daughter feels quite the opposite. It's almost as if she's wary of you. If she were in my charge, my first task would be to find out why."

The look of astonishment and disbelief on the earl's face was almost comical.

"You ascertained all of that from one short meeting?" he asked.

"I told you that was only a first impression. I could be quite wrong, my lord. Upon further understanding of them, I could easily change my mind."

"Yes, you could," he said, his voice tinged with anger. He rose from his chair and paced in front of her. It was as if he needed to walk off his annoyance. As if he needed to let his temper cool.

"Did I say something that offended you?" Emma asked.

"Of course not," his lordship snapped. "Why would you think that?"

"Just a feeling I had. Probably an incorrect one."

"I assure you, my daughters do not fear me. Nor am I partial to one over the other. I love them both equally."

"I'm sure you do," Emma said, trying to smooth over any misconstrued comments. "Please, accept my apology for anything I said that offended you."

"You did not offend me," he said through gritted teeth, and paced back and forth, then stopped in front of her. "Thank you for your honest opinion, Miss Sullivan. It was quite enlightening."

"Yet not appreciated, if I am correct?"

"You are," he said, then turned to face his daughters. "Come, girls. We've stayed long enough."

"But Papa…" Cassandra said, thinking to change her father's mind. Felicity, however, placed her napkin and silver down on the table and rose. She did not attempt to argue.

"Bid your host and hostess farewell and thank them for the lovely afternoon."

"Yes, Papa," Cassandra said, then led the way to find Janey and Isaac. Felicity followed.

Emma stepped up beside him. She wanted to make one more attempt to apologize. "I'm sorry if I was too frank, my lord."

"You were not," he answered curtly. "You were enlightening." He bowed respectfully. "Good day, Miss Sullivan," he said, then turned and walked away from her.

Emma watched his lordship leave the party with his daughters following demurely on his heels. His back was straight as an arrow and his shoulders rigid as a rifle ready to fire.

"Did you have an interesting discussion with Lord Carnhaven?" Janey asked, coming up behind Emma and placing an arm around her waist.

"He is a very confusing man, I think," Emma said.

Janey laughed. "And you do not like being confused, do you?"

"No, I do not," Emma answered. "But I think his lordship has had several years to hone his skills at hiding what he does not want people to see."

"And what do you think it is that he does not want people to see, Emma?"

"I don't know, but I am determined to find out."

SPENCER SAT IN a darkened corner of the library and finished off another snifter of brandy. He'd lost count of the number of times he'd refilled the glass, but it was more than he'd allowed himself to imbibe in a long while. Today was the second time in as many days that someone had noted the difference in how he treated his two daughters. The first time was shocking enough, since it came from Cassandra herself, when she asked how long it would take to walk to their grandmother's estate. But this afternoon was quite another blow, when Emma Sullivan, a perfect stranger, a woman who had never met Cassandra or Felicity before, saw immediately how differently he treated one daughter over the other.

Was it really so obvious? Did everyone see it? Did everyone know that he blamed Felicity for Caroline's death?

It was ugly of him, and he knew it. But God help him, he was helpless to feel otherwise.

He knew he was not equipped to be both mother and father to his daughters. Perhaps if Caroline had given him two sons he wouldn't feel quite so alone and ill prepared, but she hadn't. She'd given him daughters to raise.

Spencer reached for the brandy decanter again and refilled his glass. He'd lifted it halfway to his mouth when the door opened a crack and a sliver of light crept across the darkened room. The door closed again, casting the room in temporary darkness. A few seconds later the intruder lit a lamp and a small part of the room glowed softly.

Spencer sat back in his chair and did his best not to make a sound. He didn't know who was creeping around at this time of night, but if it was a thief, he wanted to catch him or her in the act.

A second later, the library's stepladder was unfolded, and the intruder climbed upward. Spencer stood and walked toward the ladder. "May I be of assistance, my lady?"

The female at the top of the ladder squealed in fright, then turned. She lost her balance, toppled from the ladder, and fell into his arms.

"Felicity?" he asked, looking at the small girl whose lovely hair tumbled over his arm. She was a sweet little replica of her mother, and he was struck again by her beauty. "What were you up to?"

"I was up the ladder, Papa, up to the top shelf."

Spencer chuckled. "I'm well aware, little lass. But why?"

He was shocked to see her wide eyes fill with fear.

"I'm... I'm sorry, Pa... Papa," she stuttered. "I... I didn't know... you were... I was... Sorry!"

"Don't apologize, Felicity. This is your house. You have every right to be here," he replied, trying to soften the stern quality that had crept into his voice. He sat his young daughter down on the chair where he'd been sitting. "What are you doing up so late?"

Her gaze lowered to the floor. "I couldn't sleep, so I came down to get a book to read."

Spencer's gaze followed hers and locked on a massive tome that had fallen to the floor. "Is this the book you intended to read?"

"Ye... yes, Papa."

"Do you know what this book is called, Felicity?"

"Yes, Papa. It's *The Count of Monte Cristo*. See?" She laid a small hand on the book's cover. "I like the stories Mr. Alexandre Dumas tells."

Spencer swallowed hard, finding it oddly challenging to draw a breath. His young daughter had not only chosen a book from his library that children her age would normally not even be aware of, but she knew its title and the name of its author.

"Have you read anything else written by Mr. Dumas?"

"Yes, Papa. I just finished *The Three Musketeers*. It was quite interesting. Then I overheard two ladies in the Page Turner Bookshop discussing *The Count of Monte Cristo*, and one of them said this book was much better than *The Three Musketeers*. So, I wanted to read it next."

"That's quite ambitious of you, Felicity."

"I tried reading the books I'm supposed to read, but I find them quite boring, Father. I enjoy more... Um..."

"Adventurous?" Spencer added for her.

"Yes, Papa. More adventurous stories."

"Would you read to me for a bit?"

"You would like *me* to read to *you*?"

"Yes, Felicity. Just a page or two. It's been several years since I read it. Just remind me of the story and perhaps we can discuss it sometime."

"Of course, Papa."

Felicity took the book in her hands, then climbed onto his lap and began to read. To say Spencer was impressed with her reading skills was an understatement. She read as well, if not better, than Cassandra, who was almost three years her senior.

She needed help with the geographical names and immediately asked Spencer where Cape Margiou was. Immediately charmed by her curiosity, he turned to the map he'd seen on the book's flyleaf and explained the cape's proximity to England. He was astonished at how quickly she grasped the information.

One page turned into two, then three, and finally Spencer told her she could stop. Rarely had she had to ask him for help pronouncing a word.

"You are an excellent reader, Felicity," he said.

"Thank you, Papa. I love to read."

"I'm glad you do. Reading has always been one of my favorite things to do."

"I'm so glad we have such a fine library. It's almost as fun to come here to choose a book as it is to go to the Page Turner."

"Yes, I can see where it would be. Now, I think it's time you returned to bed."

"Very well, Papa."

"But don't stay up too much longer, Felicity."

"I won't, Papa." His daughter slid off his lap and walked to the door. "Good night, Papa."

"Good night, Felicity."

She looked at him once more before she opened the door and slipped from the room. Spencer was cloaked in darkness again. Except the darkness didn't seem nearly as all-consuming. His daughter had given him a glimmer of light to hold on to.

CHAPTER FIVE

SPENCER ROSE EARLY the next morning, even though he'd managed to get very little sleep the night before. All he thought about was the startling revelation that his daughter had a fantastic ability to read. He wondered if her talents extended to other areas, such as science, or history, or even math. He wouldn't be surprised if they did.

He was an advanced reader himself at a very young age. He was also quite advanced in history and math, although he wasn't so proficient in science. Perhaps because he didn't enjoy it so much.

The question was...what was he to do to advance Felicity's abilities?

He walked to the stable and saddled his horse. Mounting quickly, he rode out with no certain destination in mind. He only needed to think. To come up with an answer to this perplexing problem.

What had his parents done to assist him in his studies?

The answer came as sharply as a bolt of lightning out of the blue. They'd hired a tutor to guide him.

It wasn't the thing to hire a tutor for females, but quite common to hire a governess to assist young ladies in becoming proper young women who would fit into Society.

One name rose to the forefront of possible governesses, but it was not a name he wished to consider.

He urged his horse into a full gallop, hoping he could outrun his problems, but alas, no matter how fast he pushed his horse, the problem remained front and center in his mind. He needed to get a governess for his daughters, and in his mind he knew Emma Sullivan was the perfect choice. She had all the qualifications he would require. She was intelligent and knew a great deal about a wide variety of topics. She had a keen, probing mind. And she understood young girls.

Spencer slowed his horse, then brought him to a halt and dismounted near a meandering brook. While his horse drank, Spencer sat on an outcrop of rock to think. Everything about Miss Sullivan was perfect, it seemed. He scarcely wanted to admit it to himself, but his only reservation was how she put his libido in utter turmoil.

It had been more than five years since Caroline had died, and in all that time he'd never noticed another woman. He hadn't found another female attractive, or been drawn to one the way he was drawn to Miss Sullivan. Nor had his body reacted to one the way it did to her.

If he hired her to be governess to his daughters, he would have to avoid her as much as he could. He'd have to stay as far away from her as possible.

Spencer mounted his horse and rode back to Carnhaven Manor. Once his horse was stabled, he retired to his room to bathe and dress in clothes appropriate for calling on a lady. When he was ready, he mounted a fresh horse and rode the short distance to Reynolds House.

"My lord," Isaac's butler greeted him. "What a pleasant surprise, but I'm afraid his lordship isn't at home. He's at his office."

"That's quite all right, Jenkins. I'm here to speak with Miss Sullivan. Might she be available?"

"I will see, your lordship."

The butler showed him to a drawing room, then left him.

Spencer paced the room like a nervous schoolboy called to

the headmaster's office, then made himself at home and sat in one of the cushioned chairs.

He didn't have to wait long before Jenkins returned. He opened the door and stepped into the room. "Miss Emma Sullivan," he announced.

Spencer rose and watched the lady enter the room.

Something leaped inside him when he saw her. He wasn't pleased with the reaction she caused, and his breath caught in his throat. "Miss Sullivan," he greeted her, bowing respectfully.

"Lord Carnhaven," she said, and bobbed politely. "Please be seated."

Spencer waited until she took a seat before he sat. When she did, he couldn't drag his eyes away.

Her gown was the perfect shade of peach to contrast with her dark blonde hair and brown eyes. She wore a frown, as if his appearance confused her, but there was a glimmer in her eyes that caused him to breathe more quickly.

"Lord Carnhaven, to what do I owe the pleasure of your visit?"

"Miss Sullivan, I have come to discuss a personal matter with you."

The surprise on her face was evident. "A personal matter?"

"Yes. It concerns my daughters."

"Your daughters?"

"Yes. Felicity in particular."

"I see."

Spencer watched the frown deepen across Miss Sullivan's forehead. He clutched his hands to keep them from reaching out to smooth the furrows. It was what he wanted to do to ease her worry.

"There is nothing wrong with Felicity. She is quite all right. My concern is her advanced skills."

"I'm afraid I don't understand. I know from the little time I spent with her the other day that she is quite intelligent, and advanced in several areas, but I'm not sure I would consider her advanced skills a concern. Could you please elaborate?"

Spencer locked his gaze with Miss Sullivan's and noticed several traits he'd overlooked before. He'd never noticed the streaks of red in her hair when the sunlight shone through the window and glistened in the curling tendrils. Nor had he noticed the few freckles that wandered across her nose.

"You were going to elaborate, my lord," she said softly.

"Yes." Spencer rose from his chair and walked a few paces beyond her. "Two nights ago I went to my library quite late. After I'd been there a while, the door opened, and Felicity entered the room. It was far past her bedtime, and I couldn't imagine what had kept her up. As it happened, she had come to retrieve a book. She said she couldn't sleep and wanted something to read."

"And you found that odd?"

"No, no," he answered. "It wasn't that she wanted something to read. It was *what* she chose to read that surprised me. Do you know what book she chose?"

Miss Sullivan's lips lifted to form the most startling smile he'd ever seen, and her sparkling eyes seemed to light the space between her chair and his.

"Would I be correct in suggesting she chose *The Count of Monte Cristo*?"

Spencer couldn't hide his shock. "How did you know?"

"Because she asked me if I'd ever heard of it when we chatted the other day. I told her that not only had I heard of it, but that I'd already read it and I found it exciting."

Spencer slumped back into his chair. He knew he looked quite undignified, but was there nothing about Emma Sullivan that didn't shock and befuddle him?

"I have only read two of Mr. Dumas's works," she said, "although I have to admit I enjoyed *The Count of Monte Cristo* the best."

"Don't you consider that particular book a bit advanced for a child of eight?"

"I find it extremely advanced for an eight-year-old, my lord.

But I believe it to be appropriate for your daughter's level of intellectual sophistication. You have a remarkable little mind on your hands, sir."

"So, what would you suggest I do with a daughter like Felicity?"

Miss Sullivan thought a few moments. "Do you want my honest opinion, my lord?"

"I do. That is why I came to see you."

"Very well, then. I think you have two options."

"And they are?"

"You can send her to a private boarding school—a carefully chosen one—where they will work with her talents and abilities. Or…"

Spencer shook his head. Caroline would never have agreed to send Felicity away at such an early age. She would have done anything in her power to keep their daughter at home until she was old enough to go to a finishing school.

"I'm afraid that is not an option," he said. "She is far too young."

"Very well. Then I would consider hiring a governess to work with her—with her and Cassandra."

"But Cassandra doesn't have the same abilities Felicity has."

"Perhaps not. But there is no point in leaving her behind and confirming the point that she is not as advanced. Cassandra may not read as competently as Felicity, but she has abilities that need to be developed."

"Of course she does," Spencer said, before he stood and paced the floor in agitation.

He couldn't believe he was having this conversation. How had his daughters grown up so quickly? They were just babies a few days ago. Now, he was considering a governess for Cassandra to prepare her for her come-out, and for Felicity to honor and challenge her academic skills. Where had the time gone? And what was he going to do about it?

Spencer stopped pacing and looked Miss Sullivan in the eyes.

The answer was staring him in the face. He needed a governess for his daughters, and the perfect governess was sitting before him. If only she didn't present such a threat to his emotions. If only his body didn't react to her like it did.

"Miss Sullivan, may I ask if you will consider being governess to my daughters?"

Her face was lined with confusion and her mouth opened several times, yet no sound came out. "I… I'm afraid I… I could not, Lord Carnhaven."

She stood, then walked away from him. Before she reached too great a distance, she turned to face him. "I'm dreadfully sorry, Lord Carnhaven. But I cannot."

EMMA SAW HOW surprised he was by her answer, yet she could not reconsider. She could not change her mind. There was a possibility that she could be charged with murder. She may have killed Lord Slushman.

She could not have a close association with the Earl of Carnhaven. If what she'd done was discovered, it would bring shame upon his family. Not only would Lord Carnhaven be ruined, but his daughters would pay the price for what Emma had done. They might even be cast out of Society and never allowed to make advantageous matches.

"Are you going to offer me an explanation, Miss Sullivan?"

"I'm sorry, my lord, but I cannot. I am not at liberty to explain my reasons for refusing your offer. The reasons are mine, and mine alone. But…" Emma paused, suddenly wanting to tell him and at the same time not daring to. "But if you knew my reasons, I have no doubt you would concur."

"I see," his lordship answered. "Is there anything I can do or say to change your mind?"

Emma felt the sting of tears. "No, my lord. There is nothing."

"Am I the reason you have refused me? Did I offend you so greatly at Isaac and Miss Franklin's reception?"

"No, my lord. You did not offend me. In fact, I thoroughly enjoyed our conversation."

"Then why? Is it Felicity? I know she can be—"

"Felicity would be the reason I *would* accept your offer, my lord. She would be a joy to work with. A joy to teach, and a student to whom I could open up a world of new horizons. She is on the brink of finding new worlds to explore."

"Then I don't understand, Miss Sullivan."

The first tear streamed down her cheek. "I know you don't, my lord. And I pray you will accept my lack of explanation. It is all I am at liberty to offer."

"Then I am forced to accept your decision, Miss Sullivan." The Earl of Carnhaven rose and bowed politely. "I will see myself out," he said, and exited the room.

Emma let the tears fall from her eyes. Her decision had been for the best. She'd had no other choice. If she elected to be governess to his daughters and were charged with murder, it would cause a scandal from which his daughters would never recover. And even if she was never discovered, the risks were too great to ignore.

There was an attraction to Lord Carnhaven that Emma couldn't deny. It was only a matter of time before one of them acted on that attraction, and that would be equally as devastating as her being charged with murder. That would also ruin his life and his reputation.

No, she had no choice. As soon as Janey and Isaac married, she had to leave Willowbrook and make a life for herself someplace far away from here. Someplace where she could not ruin more lives than she already had.

CHAPTER SIX

FOR DAYS, SPENCER replayed his conversation with Emma Sullivan over and over in his mind, and with each revisit he was more confused. What was keeping her from accepting his offer to be governess to his daughters? It couldn't be that she had money no one knew about. When they arrived, Isaac told him they had made it as far as Willowbrook because that was as far as their money could take them.

Spencer rose from his chair and refilled his glass of brandy. This was a puzzle he couldn't solve, and something inside him continued to nag at him until he had an answer to his question.

He walked to his desk and took out a piece of stationery. There was only one person who might know the answer to his question—only one who might tell him—and that was Isaac. But Spencer couldn't go to see Isaac. Miss Sullivan was there, and he didn't want her to know that he'd spoken to Isaac, or risk her overhearing their conversation. No, he had to ask his friend to come to Carnhaven.

He penned a quick note and called for a footman to have it delivered. Hopefully, he would have his answer before the day was out.

ISAAC ARRIVED EVEN sooner than Spencer expected. Once he assured his friend there was no dire emergency, Spencer poured each of them a snifter of brandy, then sat down. "Thank you for coming so quickly, Isaac. I hope I haven't spoiled your day."

"Is something wrong, Spence?"

"No, not wrong, exactly."

"Then what is it?"

"I caught Felicity sneaking into the library in the middle of the night. She'd come for a book."

"Do you consider that so unusual?"

"No, but what I consider unusual is the book she chose. *The Count of Monte Cristo*."

"The Dumas novel?"

Spencer nodded, then took a sip of his brandy. "She's only eight years old, Isaac. When I questioned her about it, she told me she just finished reading *The Three Musketeers* and wanted to read *Monte Cristo* next."

"Bloody hell," Isaac said with a frown. "What did you say to her?"

"Well, my first impression was to question her. I didn't believe her. I didn't think it was possible for her to read something so massive and difficult, so I asked her to read the first few pages to me."

"And…?"

"She read it as if it were one of her primers."

Isaac sat there for a time without saying a word, as if he was dumbfounded. "I have to admit that I read *Monte Cristo* less than a year ago, and it took me a month or more to get through it."

"I know. Me too."

"What are you going to do?"

"My plan was to hire someone to be the girls' governess. I was going to employ someone for Cassandra now, then in a few years, allow Felicity to begin lessons. But I can see that Felicity can take advantage of someone to guide her even more than Cassandra might."

"Do you have someone in mind?"

"I thought I did, but she refused my offer."

"You are talking about Emma, aren't you."

"I am."

"Did she give you a reason?" Isaac asked.

"No. That's why I wanted to speak with you. Do you know why she would refuse me?"

Isaac rose and brought the decanter of brandy to refill Spencer's glass as well as his own. "I do, Spence, but I'm not at liberty to say."

"Why?"

"Because I was told in the strictest of confidence."

"Please, help me to understand, Isaac."

"Truly, my friend, I cannot. All I can do is encourage you to speak to Emma again and implore her to help you, for Felicity's sake."

"Do you think she might change her mind?" Spencer asked.

"I think there is a possibility. Janey is afraid Emma will leave Willowbrook as soon as we're married."

"Why would she leave? Her only friend is here."

"To *protect* her only friend. That's why."

"You're not making sense. How would leaving Willowbrook protect Janey?"

Isaac took a long swallow of his drink. "You're an intelligent man, Spence. Why would you leave your best friend to protect them?"

Spencer rose to his feet and paced the room, then stopped in front of Isaac. "What has she done that is so terrible that she fears for the safety of those around her?"

"You will have to ask her that question, Spence. She's the only one who can give you an answer."

Spencer considered Isaac's words.

"Perhaps you can call on her tomorrow afternoon. I will make sure Janey is out of the house, and Emma will be alone."

"Thank you, my friend. I appreciate your help."

⋙⋘

EMMA SAT IN the library with an open book in her hands, but she couldn't concentrate on the words long enough to keep her mind on the story. Janey and Isaac had set their wedding for the following Friday. She had less than a week until they would wed, and within days after that Emma would have to settle on where she would go.

Oh, Janey would employ every power of persuasion at her disposal to try to convince Emma to stay, but she couldn't do that. There was nothing more unwelcome than a third wheel living in the same house with a newly married bride and groom.

No, she would have to leave while Janey and Isaac were on their honeymoon. She would only be in the way.

Emma knew what she had to do. Except she dreaded doing it. Where would she go? What would she do? What if someone recognized her?

She closed her book and placed it on her lap when there was a knock on the door and she had something else to concentrate on.

"Yes?"

One of the maids opened the door. "You have a gentleman caller, Miss Emma."

"Are you sure it's for me?"

"Yes, Miss Emma. It's the Earl of Carnhaven. He specifically asked for you."

"Send him in, Janet. And please bring in a tea tray."

"Right away, miss."

Emma wondered what his lordship wanted. She thought she'd made her refusal plain earlier when she told him there was no way she could stay here and be governess to his daughters, even though that would be the perfect answer to her problem—at least until someone discovered who she was and what she'd done. Or until the authorities came to arrest her for the murder of Lord Slushman, and Lord Carnhaven and his daughters were embroiled in a scandal.

Emma heard footsteps approach the library door and stood.

Janet opened the door and introduced their guest. "Lord Carnhaven to see you, miss."

"Th-thank you, Janet," Emma stammered nervously. "Please, come in, my lord," she managed to say. "Have a seat. Tea should be here momentarily."

"Thank you, Miss Sullivan." Lord Carnhaven entered the room and stood by a chair. He waited for Emma to sit, then followed suit. "I know this is a surprise, but I could not help but make one more attempt to convince you to teach my daughters what they need to know to get along in life."

"Lord Carnhaven, I already explained—"

"I know what you told me, Miss Sullivan, but I'm afraid your explanation was inadequate."

"Inadequate?"

"What I mean," he said, "is that I don't accept your explanation. In other words, I think there are several details you left out that would have cleared up your story."

Thankfully, Janet rolled in the tea tray just then and poured. When she finished, she left quietly and Emma was alone with Lord Carnhaven again.

"If I recall correctly from a conversation I had with Miss Franklin shortly after you arrived, the reason you ended up in Willowbrook was because this was all the money you had for coach fare. Is that correct?"

Emma knew he was leading her into a trap. "Yes, my lord."

"If that was all the money you had, how have you been living since you arrived?"

"Isaac has been very generous with his time and his money. He has given us a place to stay, and provided us with clothes to wear, since we arrived with none."

"And why was that?"

Emma's hand shook, and she placed her cup and saucer on the table in front of her. "That is none of your concern, my lord."

"But it is, Miss Sullivan. Isaac is my closest friend, and I would do anything to protect him and keep him from getting harmed."

"You think I would harm him after all he's done for us? Or do you think Janey would? I assure you she would not. She loves him. She intends to marry him."

"Yes, and he loves her. But does he know everything there is to know about her?"

"Yes. He knows everything."

"Then it's only a matter of time until I convince him to tell me everything."

"He won't. He promised he would not."

"Do you think it's fair for him to shoulder your burden, and his wife's burden, by himself?"

"We have no choice," Emma answered.

"You do, Miss Sullivan. You can tell me what trouble you and Janey are in. I am not without a certain amount of influence, and I will do everything in my power to protect you."

Before Emma could stop them, tears filled her eyes and spilled down her cheeks.

"Let me help you, Miss Sullivan."

"I can't."

"You can. I promise I will help you."

"Why? Why would you help me?"

"Because I need you to help me."

Emma wiped her eyes. "And if I don't?"

"Then I will make a trip to London and find your last place of employment. I will talk to your former employers and gather all the information I can about you and Janey. Is that what you want?"

Emma's heart thundered in her breast and her breathing turned into gasps of air.

"Is it?"

"No!"

"Then tell me what I want to know."

Emma wanted to run away from him. She wanted to escape

him and go someplace where he wouldn't be. Someplace where she would be safe. But there was nowhere to go.

She bolted to her feet and took one step away from him, but her legs refused to support her and she lost her balance.

He quickly reached out for her. "Hold on to me, my lady." He gripped her at the waist and held her tight. "Come with me. You need to sit down."

Emma allowed him to lead her to the sofa. "I'm sorry. That was silly of me."

"Not silly, Emma. Understandable. Whatever you're hiding is a heavy weight on your shoulders. Won't you share your burden with me? Please."

Emma lifted her chin and locked her gaze with his. She tried to remain strong, but his arms supporting her made her want to give in to him and let him be her strength.

"Please, Emma. Tell me what burden you're carrying and let me help you."

"Once I tell you, Lord Carnhaven, you will hate me. I am not proud of what I did. It is nothing a gently bred lady should ever do."

"I promise, Emma. I will never hate you. Never."

Emma settled onto the sofa and clutched her hands in her lap. For some unexplainable reason, she needed to tell him what she'd done. She couldn't keep her secret to herself any longer. She had to tell someone. Someone who might understand.

"I will not blame you if you hate me for what I've done, but at least you will know the kind of person I am and cease asking me to teach your daughters. You will know why I am the least qualified person to be anywhere near Cassandra and Felicity."

The Earl of Carnhaven reached for her hands clutched in her lap and held them. "Tell me and let me be the judge of that. I will make up my own mind."

Emma knew he was right. She had no choice but to let him decide for himself what kind of person she was. She kept her hands clenched in his and took a deep breath, then started her tale.

"Janey and I were employed by the Earl and Countess of Pearlman in London. They were demanding employers, but good people to work for. Their son, Viscount Slushman, however, was the lowest of creatures."

"I have heard that he is a lecher and that he abuses the staff. Especially the female staff members."

"That is all true. He corners any female staff member he takes a fancy to and has his way with them. The minute they become pregnant, he dismisses them and we never see them again."

"I see," Carnhaven said. "Are his parents aware of his actions?"

"I'm sure they are, but he is their only son and the Pearlman heir. They refuse to believe the rumors pertaining to him."

"How sad." Carnhaven took a long breath. "So. Where is the child?"

Emma looked up sharply. "What child?"

He patted her hand. "*Your* child. The one Slushman forced upon you. The one you're too ashamed for me to know about."

"Oh dear God! There is no child!"

"No child? But then why—"

"Because I murdered him!" Emma covered her face with her hands. She'd said it. Now he knew. What should be feeling like shame felt more like relief.

"My God. How?"

Emma swiped the tears from her cheeks and grappled for composure. If he wanted the sordid details, she had plenty to provide.

"Janey and I were always able to protect each other from Slushman's advances…until the night we fled London."

"What happened that night?"

"I had just checked on my charges to make sure they were asleep when I heard Janey scream. I ran to her as quickly as I could and found Lord Slushman about to rape her."

Lord Carnhaven slid closer, wrapped his arm around her

shoulders, and pulled her to him. Emma leaned her head on his chest and let him hold her.

"Go on."

"I ran into my room and retrieved a letter opener. I ran back to Janey and fought Slushman with all my strength, but he refused to release her, so I…"

Tears streamed down Emma's cheeks. She couldn't stop them. She was reliving that night as if it were happening anew.

"It's all right, Emma. You're safe." He cupped her face and wiped the tears that streamed down her cheeks. Then he retrieved a handkerchief from his pocket and offered it to her. "You're safe here. Don't worry anymore."

"I can't help it, my lord. I think I might have…"

"What? What do you think you might have done?"

"I think I might have killed him," she said, sobbing. "I stabbed him several times. He fell to the floor and didn't move again. Janey and I threw our meager belongings into a bag and gathered the little money we had, and I purchased tickets on the mail coach to Willowbrook. I used nearly all the money I had. Luckily, when we arrived here, Isaac recognized Janey and he offered us sanctuary."

"Have you heard any further news on the condition of Viscount Slushman?"

Emma shook her head. "I comb through the *Times* and other gossip papers that Isaac brings home from his office, but haven't seen any further news concerning Viscount Slushman."

"Perhaps he recovered."

"Perhaps," Emma replied. "Although I'm not sure what is worse—knowing he's dead and having to wait for his father to send men from Scotland Yard to arrest me, or knowing he's alive and living in fear that he will search for me to exact his revenge."

"And you truly believe you'll be safer on your own?" Lord Carnhaven asked, turning her to look her in the eyes.

Emma pulled her hands from his grasp. "No. I won't be safer. But you and your daughters will be safer with me far away from you, and Isaac and Janey and everyone in Willowbrook will be safer. Staying here will only put all of you in danger."

"Let me take care of that. I will protect you. I will make sure nothing happens to you or anyone around you. Pack your belongings and come to my house the minute Janey and Isaac are married. You'll be safe there. I won't let anything happen to you."

Chapter Seven

Emma smiled as tears filled her eyes when Janey and Isaac pledged their vows and became man and wife. The smile on Janey's face was something to behold. She was truly happy for the first time since Emma had known her. And the look in Isaac's eyes showed more love and devotion than Emma had ever seen.

The happy bride and groom left the church with Emma and Lord Carnhaven following behind. Emma couldn't help but scan the congregation for any strangers who looked like they didn't belong. Thankfully, there was no one who reminded her of Viscount Slushman.

At the reception, she greeted the happy newlyweds, then watched as they took to the floor for the opening dance.

"They make a handsome couple, don't they?" Carnhaven said, standing close beside her.

"Yes, they do."

"How are you doing, Emma?"

Emma took note of his familiar use of her name. No more Miss Sullivan. Simply Emma. She felt oddly comforted by it. He was not forward in his tone, but came across more as if speaking to her as an equal.

"I'm doing well, thank you. I'm glad the wedding is over and Janey is married. It offers her a modicum of protection, don't you think?"

"Yes. Now she has the protection of a husband and his title. That's very important. What about you?"

"Me?"

"Yes, you. Have you decided what you're going to do?"

Emma turned toward Lord Carnhaven. She wanted to see his face when she told him what she had decided. Some people were more difficult to read than others. Lord Carnhaven was one of those. He hid his emotions extremely well, but there were one or two telltale signs that indicated what he was thinking. The most obvious was the muscle in his jaw. It clenched and rippled when he disagreed with something she said, or when she said something that made him angry.

"Would you care to take some air? Isaac has such lovely grounds."

"Yes, I would," he answered. "It's a perfect day for it."

Lord Carnhaven extended his arm, and Emma placed her hand atop his sleeve. Her fingers trembled for a moment, then calmed. There was something terrifying about the strength he emitted, yet something about the masterful way he controlled everything around him that made her feel safe and secure.

She couldn't keep herself from turning her head and looking up. Her gaze met his, and she smiled.

"What?" he asked.

She shook her head. "Nothing. It's just that I doubt you are even aware of the power you emit."

"Power?" He gave a hearty laugh that caused Emma's entire body to warm.

"Yes, power and strength."

"Oh my," he said. "You need to cease with the accolades, or you will cause me to think more of myself than is warranted."

"I doubt that is possible," Emma said as they turned down a pebbled path in the garden. "You are far too humble and modest to think yourself so important."

"I see," he said, leading her to a secluded gazebo at the crest of another path. "And to what do you attribute my humility?"

Emma sat on a wooden bench tucked next to the railing that skirted the perimeter of the gazebo, but didn't speak for a moment.

"Yes?" he encouraged her when she didn't answer immediately.

Emma turned her head to face him. "I attribute your humility to the great loss you endured in your life. Before you lost your wife, you were a man who had the ability to control everything around you. Everything except life and death. You learned that no matter how much power you wield, there are some things you cannot control. Death is one of those things."

With a look of shock and surprise, Lord Carnhaven rose to his feet. He stepped to the railing and lowered his head between his outstretched arms.

Emma feared she'd gone too far, that she'd opened up wounds she had no right to pry into.

"Is there a reason you are speaking with such cruelty and heartless frankness?" he asked.

"I'm sorry if I spoke out of turn, but I feel it's important that you stop blaming yourself for your wife's death—and that you stop blaming Felicity. You did everything in your power to save her, and Felicity was just a baby."

"Blaming Felicity? What do you know about that day? It was *me*. I was the one who didn't save her mother. When she's old enough to realize that, she'll hate me. You know *nothing* about that day!"

Emma shook her head. "I know what I've heard. I know that whenever anyone talks about your wife, they speak of what a great love you had. That you were the happiest of couples, but a part of you died with her. And some of that blame transferred to Felicity."

"That's absurd! Why would you say that?"

"Because you keep your daughter at an arm's length. You've just said that when she's older she'll blame you. She'll hate you. So if you don't love her too much now, it won't hurt so badly when she turns her back on you. My lord, she was just a baby when your wife drowned. There was nothing she could have done then to save her mother, and nothing she can do now to save you. Don't you think she sees that? And every time you push her away—"

"Stop!" Carnhaven growled. "There was nothing she could have done, but there was something I could have done. I could have saved her mother. I could have saved them both!"

He stood at the railing for a long while, then wiped at his eyes. Emma watched his shoulders heave and struggled to keep her distance.

"I'm sorry, my lord. You are right. I spoke cruelly and with heartless frankness. But I thought it was important that I make you understand how important it is that you saved Felicity's life and that you no longer allow her mother's death to come between you."

Lord Carnhaven didn't immediately turn to face her, but when he did, his face showed clearly the emotional upset she'd caused.

"You don't intend to stay, do you, Miss Sullivan? That's why you are so blunt, isn't it?"

"I can't, my lord. Everyone around me will be in danger if I do."

"I couldn't keep my wife safe, so I couldn't keep *you* safe. Is that it?"

Emma closed her eyes and shook her head. "No, my lord. Not at all! It's because I don't underestimate Lord Slushman's viciousness and cruelty. It's because I recognize the inherent evil that is buried deep inside the man. I see no redeeming quality living within him. Not one. He is a man to be feared and avoided at all cost."

"So, you will leave us rather than risk facing his wrath. Never mind what a fluke it would be for him to actually find you."

"I must, don't you see?"

Lord Carnhaven looked at her for a long moment. The anger

and hopelessness slowly drained from his face. The muscle along his jaw no longer clenched and rippled. He sighed heavily and spread his hands wide.

"Is there anything I can say to change your mind?"

His voice was soft, his eyes beseeching her to reconsider.

"No, my lord. My mind is firmly made up."

"That I can see," he said, taking a step closer to her. Emma knew she should take a step away from him, but it was as if her feet refused to follow her instructions. Even when he reached out and caressed her cheek, she could not move away.

His palm cradled her cheek, and she couldn't take in a breath. Her body refused to work.

"Promise me one thing, will you? Please?"

"Yes, my lord," she said in a breathy whisper. "What is it?"

"Wherever you are, if Slushman has followed you, send word and I will come."

"Of course. I will send for you."

Without warning, Lord Carnhaven lowered his head and pressed his lips to hers. His kiss was soft and tender, demanding nothing in return. Only the promise of things to come.

He kissed her one more time, then wrapped his arms around her and held her again. She pulled away from him and turned her back. It took all the strength she had and left her a weak, broken imitation of the person she had been just moments earlier.

"Goodbye, Emma," he said with a thick voice.

"Goodbye, my lord," she managed to say, and forced herself to move away from the first man she felt she might have actually been able to love.

Chapter Eight

Emma was leaving in the morning. She had so few possessions that it took just one hatbox, a soft satchel, and a child's trunk to hold her worldly goods. It had taken less than an hour to organize what little she would be taking with her.

Isaac had helped her out more than she could ever repay. He'd loaned her enough money to get by until she found a position as a governess. He'd also paid her coach fare to anywhere she wanted to go. And, most importantly, he had written her a sterling letter of recommendation.

Emma still didn't know where she would go, except that it would be even farther away from London.

She'd crawled into bed a little while ago hoping to get a few hours of sleep before it was time to leave. Thankfully, she'd fallen right to sleep, only to be wakened a short while later by noise coming from downstairs—a pounding on the front door.

"Isaac!" a voice bellowed. "Is she here?"

Emma heard Isaac race down the hall, then down the stairs. "Who, Spence? Is who here?"

"Felicity! Is Felicity here?"

Emma jumped out of bed, threw her robe around her shoulders, and stepped into her slippers. She ran from her room and descended the stairs as rapidly as she could.

"Are you sure she's not in your house?" Isaac asked.

"I'm sure. We've searched every room. Even the cellar. She's gone. Cassandra doesn't know where she is either. Good God, Isaac. She's only eight years old. Where could she have gone?"

"Has she mentioned wanting to go someplace?"

"No. She isn't talking to me at the moment."

"Why not?" Emma asked, reaching the bottom of the stairs.

"We had a falling out. A disagreement."

"Over what?"

"Something trivial. I criticized the amount of time she spent tracing pictures instead of drawing freehand. It was stupid of me!"

"I see," Emma said. "What about Cassandra? Has Felicity mentioned to her sister that she wanted to go someplace?"

"No. Wait, yes! Cassandra said Felicity wanted to know how far it was to their grandmother's."

"Your mother's house?"

"No, Caroline's mother's estate."

"What did you tell her?"

"That it was too far away, and that it was too dangerous for her to travel there. That there were footpads and robbers and someone who would try to kidnap her and hold her for ransom."

"That's where we'll find her, then. Along the road to her grandmother's."

"Do you really think so?"

"I do."

Lord Carnhaven swiped his hand down his face. "But surely she's not brave enough to go alone. Especially in the dark. Caroline was terrified of the dark. We had to keep a lamp lit all night for her."

"Felicity might look like her mother on the outside, but she exhibits several of your more independent traits."

"I need to go after her," the earl said, turning toward the door.

Emma looked to where Janey stood at the top of the stairs. "Please, bring down my cloak," she said, slipping on her boots from the hall cupboard. Janey ran back to Emma's room and came down the stairs with her cloak. Isaac followed closely behind her. He was dressed and wore a heavy coat.

"Are you ready?" he asked as he took Emma's arm and followed Spencer from the house. They stepped into the Earl of Carnhaven's open carriage and were off at a rapid clip.

"You were right, Emma," the Earl of Carnhaven said as they scoured the road it seemed logical that Felicity would have taken. "The child is oversensitive to my reprimands. I should have seen it before!"

His gaze shifted from one side of the road to the other. Isaac managed the horses as they sped through the dark countryside.

"I take no pleasure in being correct," Emma said.

Spencer spared her a look. "But if you were?"

Emma thought a moment. "What exactly did you say to her?"

He rubbed a hand across his brow. "I... I don't... I told her to go play outside if she wasn't going to do anything really productive."

Emma blanched. The man truly didn't realize the power of his words on a child whose one wish in life was to please him.

"Then it's possible Felicity interprets your reprimand to mean you want her out of your sight."

"Oh God." The poor man was sinking in misery. "She's such a reminder of Caroline...and I loved her so much that it hurts sometimes to see the child looking at me with my wife's eyes. I was too harsh! I know I was!"

"Then you must continually tell yourself that it's not Felicity's fault that she is a little replica of her mother. You must take pleasure in that reminder, and not punish your daughter for the legacy she so visibly carries."

"There she is!" Isaac shouted, pointing ahead of them.

The earl leaned forward to jump from the carriage, but Emma placed her hand on his arm to stop him. "Let me go to her. She's probably afraid that you're angry with her."

"I *am* angry with her."

Emma tugged at his arm. "Then I suggest you take a second look at what's really in your heart. I think anger has nothing to do with what you're feeling."

Emma stepped from the carriage and pulled her cloak tightly around her. When she caught her balance, she walked to Felicity at a more rapid pace than the tired little girl was able to keep.

"Felicity?" she called out calmly.

"Leave me alone, Miss Sullivan."

"You know I can't do that, Felicity."

"Why not? Papa can. He doesn't want me. No one does."

"But he *does*. He's sitting in the carriage. He's been searching all night for you. He's terribly worried about you."

"No he's not. He only concerns himself with Cassie."

Emma walked quietly alongside Felicity, and if the little girl would just stop for a moment, she would reach out and touch her. "Why do you think that? Why do you think he's more partial to Cassie than you?"

"Because she looks like him, and I remind him of Mama."

Oh the dear child! She's been terribly hurt.

"Do you think that's a bad thing? Do you think he didn't like your mama?" Emma put her hand on the child's shoulder and gently forced her to stop. She wrapped Felicity in her arms and held her. The sweet lass was sobbing now, and big, wet tears streamed down her cheeks.

"Oh, no. He loved Mama. He told us once how much he loved Mama."

"Then why do you think he doesn't love you?" Emma sat on the edge of the road with Felicity in her lap.

"I don't know. I try to be just like her. I try to make him love me, but I can't. Nothing I do makes him like me."

"What if I told you that your papa loves you dearly?"

"I wouldn't believe you, Miss Sullivan. He doesn't love me. I know he does not."

"Then you would be wrong, Felicity. I love you more that I can ever say," the Earl of Carnhaven's rich, velvety voice said from behind them. "I have always loved you. I love everything about you. Especially the things that remind me of your mother."

"No, you don't, Papa," Felicity said, burrowing her face into Emma's breast. "That's why I'm running away. I'm running away so you don't have to see me every day. So you don't have to be reminded of Mama every time you see me."

"Do you think that will help?" Carnhaven asked.

"I don't know," Felicity answered. "I don't know what else to do."

"There is nothing else for you to do except come home with me so I can prove to you that I love you. So I can show you just how precious you are to me."

Felicity stiffened in Emma's arms, then lifted her head and looked at her with the most pleading expression Emma had ever seen in a child's eyes.

"Only if you will come home with me, Miss Sullivan."

Emma's gaze locked with Carnhaven's.

"Please, Miss Sullivan," the earl said. "We need you to be with us. *All* of us need you."

Emma cupped Felicity's head and held her securely. What was she to do? How could she live in close proximity to Lord Carnhaven after she'd been so brutally honest in her criticisms of him? After she'd revealed so many of her thoughts to him?

Yet how could she refuse him her help? How could she abandon a small child who would feel so alone if Emma refused their plea for help?

Emma took a deep breath and slowly released it. She knew before she said even one word that she was making the biggest mistake of her life. She knew the day would come when she would regret staying close to Lord Carnhaven. The love he felt for his wife was something that would always stand between them.

"Very well. I'll go home with you. But I can't promise how long I will stay."

Felicity turned in Emma's arms and hugged her tightly.

"Thank you," Lord Carnhaven said, and the sincerity was evident in his voice as well as in his gaze.

"Are you ready to go home now?" Isaac asked from behind them.

"Yes," Lord Carnhaven answered, helping Emma and Felicity to their feet. "I imagine Cassandra is worried sick over her sister. She blames herself for your disappearance."

"She shouldn't," Felicity said. "I didn't even tell her I was leaving."

"That's why she blames herself. She thinks she should have been watching you closer."

"I will have to tell her I'm sorry, then." Felicity sniffed. "She doesn't have to think she needs to watch over me. I'm not a baby."

"But she's your older sister," Carnhaven said. "All older siblings feel it's their duty to watch over anyone younger than they are. And fathers feel it's their duty to watch over their children. In that regard, I have failed my responsibility, too."

Before they'd taken their first step to return home, Lord Carnhaven reached down, scooped his daughter up into his arms, and carried her to their carriage and sat with Felicity on his lap.

The little girl was fast asleep before they were a mile down the road, and the relief on her father's face was precious to behold.

THIS NIGHT HAD not turned out at all the way Emma imagined it would. The only thing she had done that was beneficial was that at least some of her clothes were already packed. All they had to do was stop at Ten Oaks, drop Isaac off, and pick up her trunk, valise, and hatbox. Anything else she needed could be sent over to Carnhaven Manor later.

When they arrived at Carnhaven, Spencer carried Felicity up

to the room she shared with Cassandra, and Emma readied her for bed. The exhausted child didn't even waken while Emma and Cassandra tucked her in. When they were finished and Cassandra had hugged her for the hundredth time, Emma turned down the lamps and left the room.

She stepped into the hall, hoping to see a maid to show her where her room might be. Instead, Lord Carnhaven stood outside the door.

"Is she asleep?" he asked.

"She didn't even wake. We tucked her in, and she didn't stir. The poor child was worn out."

"Would you mind joining me downstairs for a few minutes?"

"For a few minutes," Emma answered. "It is quite late."

"Yes, of course. I just want to speak with you for a moment, and I don't know when we'll next have a chance to talk when the girls aren't around."

Lord Carnhaven extended his arm, and Emma took it. He led her into what looked to be his study and showed her to a chair. When she was seated, he walked to a small table that held several crystal decanters and filled two glasses.

"A glass of wine for you?" He held out a small glass, and she took it gratefully.

"Oh yes. Please."

"I would like to thank you for everything you did for us tonight."

"There is no need," Emma replied. "I'm glad I could be of service."

"And I would also like to thank you for agreeing to come home with us and be governess to my daughters. Everything worked out exactly as I hoped it would, even though I know it wasn't what you wanted."

"It's for your family's safety that I'm worried. Until I know the severity of what I've done, I cannot rest easily."

"I understand," he said.

Carnhaven finished the wine in his glass, then looked at her glass and noticed that it was still partially full, so he rose and refilled his own. When he finished, he turned back to face her.

"I will make you a bargain, Miss Sullivan. I will go to London and see what I can discover concerning Viscount Slushman."

Emma was surprised by his concession. "And if you discover he is dead?"

"Then we will do nothing. You can live here in relative obscurity. No one need ever find out what happened that dreadful night."

"And if you discover he is still alive?"

"Then we will handle that matter when it arises. I wager that you are safe as long as you're here. You are less safe when you leave here and are on your own. I hope you recognize that."

"Thank you, my lord," Emma whispered. "You may be correct. I appreciate your help and concern."

"It's the least I can do."

Emma finished her wine, then rose to leave. The earl rose at the same time and reached out his hands to take hers.

She held out her hands and placed them in his. A thousand waves of electric current raced through her. It was stunning how easily this man's touch could have such a remarkable effect on her. How could just a simple touch be so potent?

"It's late, my lady," he said, locking his gaze with hers. "Please, sleep as late as you wish in the morning. You have had a stressful day."

"As have you," Emma replied. "We will begin again in the morning."

"Yes, Miss Sullivan," he said, then lifted her hands to his lips and kissed her trembling fingers.

At the touch of his lips, something she had not realized was harbored within her breast exploded like fireworks in a nighttime sky. Before she could stop a sigh from escaping her lips, he lifted his right hand and cupped her cheek.

He didn't hold it against her face long, only long enough to set flames of intense heat traveling from her head to her toes.

"Good night, Miss Sullivan."

"Good night, my lord."

Emma bobbed politely, then walked out of the room. Thankfully, an upstairs maid waited for her in the corridor and escorted her to a room that had been prepared for her.

Emma followed her up the stairs, knowing she would get very little sleep again tonight.

CHAPTER NINE

SPENCER AVOIDED SEEING Emma Sullivan as much as possible for the next few weeks, but that didn't mean he was successful in not thinking about her. She consumed his mind several times a day.

He couldn't help but wonder what she was doing, how she was managing with his daughters, and what she thought about the progress they were making. Even when he reminded himself it wasn't wise to think about her, his traitorous mind refused to pass the message on to his body. Like a vision, she overtook his thoughts and refused to leave him.

He sat in his study nearly every morning and worked on his books, then rode his land. He met with his stewards and got updates on the condition of the crops, as well as the herd sizes, the shearing of the sheep, and numbers of cattle and pigs ready to go to market.

The reports he received should have pleased him. They were excellent, but he had no one to share them with. No one to explain the successes with. If only he could discuss the progress of the estate with the one person he was sure would understand. If only he could talk to Emma.

A knock at the door shook him from his woolgathering. "Yes?"

"Miss Sullivan to see you, my lord."

"Show her in, Jasper."

"Yes, my lord."

Jasper bowed, then opened the door and motioned Emma into the room.

Spencer stood. "Please, Miss Sullivan. Have a seat."

"Thank you, my lord."

The lady sat, and Spencer noticed how much more rested she looked. She was truly an attractive lady. He'd noticed how pretty she was when he first met her, but there was something about her today that made her even more attractive. There was a glow about her that indicated she had come with a purpose. "Is something wrong, Miss Sullivan?"

"No, my lord. Nothing is wrong. In fact, everything is quite satisfactory."

"I'm glad to hear that. What can I help you with, then?"

She looked at him and smiled. "I would like to offer a suggestion, my lord."

"Of course. What is it?"

"I would like to bring your daughters to the main dining room to share a meal with you. They don't have to join you every day, nor does it have to be the same meal, but I think perhaps it would be beneficial for them as they learn proper dining etiquette."

"That is an excellent idea, Miss Sullivan. What do you suggest?"

"I think we should start simply, perhaps with one or two meals a week. Perhaps we should start out with the luncheon meal. That is less formal than dinner."

"Yes. That would be perfect."

"Very well, my lord," Emma said. She prepared to leave, but he held out his hand to stop her. "Was there something more you needed to discuss, my lord?"

"Yes, Miss Sullivan. I would like to ask about my daughters. How are they progressing?"

The governess settled back into her chair. "Remarkably well, my lord. Your daughters are both intelligent, as you well know. Cassandra is quite skilled at conversation, is a fine little artist, and she has a keen interest in the news of the day. She understands a good deal about the intricacies of Society and looks forward to the day when she will have her come-out."

Spencer was shocked. He hadn't thought of introducing Cassie to Society. She was just a little girl. "Do you think that is something that should be encouraged?"

"I believe that is a normal occurrence for someone of Cassie's class. What I don't intend to encourage is her wanting to grow up too fast."

"Nor do I, Miss Sullivan." Spencer saw a smile light up her face. "You don't seem concerned about her growing up too fast."

"I'm not, my lord. Every young lady matures differently. Some earlier. Some later. The advantage is in being cognizant of how and when each young lady matures so we can guide them in this change and warn them of the dangers of which they should be aware."

"Is this how your mother handled your formative years?"

"My mother died when I was born, so I had no one to guide me through those years. My father was too busy with his shipping ventures and estate to bother with me."

"Similar to how I ignored Felicity, wasn't it. No wonder you recognized the signs so quickly."

Emma had become noticeably uncomfortable, and Spencer didn't want that. They were getting along so well that he didn't want to ruin it.

"And what about Felicity? How is she getting along?" he asked.

"You already know that her reading is far advanced for a child her age. She is also an excellent student in several other areas."

"Such as?"

"Such as classical literature, creative writing, mathematics, and the sciences. Where Cassandra enjoys painting, watercolors, and embroidery, Felicity has very little interest in those endeavors."

"So, what do you encourage instead of the usual female pastimes?"

"I encourage her to discover opportunities to see numbers in the world around her… To discover the natural order of things, but through mathematics."

"In other words, you encourage each one of them to do what interests them most."

"Yes, my lord. I encourage them to become better at what they enjoy doing." A smile lifted the corners of her mouth.

"What is it, Miss Sullivan?"

The governess lowered her gaze to her hands locked in her lap.

"Please, Miss Sullivan. What would you like to add?"

"Well…" she said hesitantly. "It's just that your youngest daughter indicated a desire to learn something new."

"And you refused her?"

"Not exactly, my lord. I encouraged her to discuss what she wanted to do with you."

"With me?"

"Yes. It's something you would be much more knowledgeable about than I would."

Spencer couldn't help but laugh. "I can't imagine anything at which I am more proficient than you would be."

"Fishing. Your daughter would like to go fishing, my lord. You have a beautiful little lake right here, and—"

Spencer felt as if he'd been punched in the solar plexus. He hadn't gone near the lake since the day Caroline drowned. And now his daughter wanted to return to the very spot where her mother died.

"No! I forbid it!"

"I'm not sure I understand—"

"I said no! I don't want you to take my daughters anywhere near the water! Do you hear me? Stay away from that lake!"

"Yes, my lord," Emma said, then rose. "Is there anything else you wanted to say?"

"No," he answered, then reached for his glass.

Without another word, she turned and left the room.

Spencer drank from his glass and filled it again. He'd handled that all wrong, but the very thought of his daughters anywhere near the small lake set his heart clenching in his chest. He'd threatened to fill in the damned lake a hundred times over the years. Now she wanted him to invite Felicity there on a fishing lark. There was no way. No way in hell he could take her back to that place.

EMMA WAS STILL shaken from her conversation with Lord Carnhaven. She knew his temper was always close to the surface, but she didn't know how quickly it could erupt or how violent it could become. But she was determined to get this troubled man and his daughters past this barricade, or they might never experience the love he kept locked away. All because of the blasted tragedy none of them could have averted.

As Emma pondered the dilemma, an idea began to slowly take shape. On her next half-day off, she would call on Janey and hope Isaac was there. She would get his opinion as to how to coax her employer into complying with his daughter's wish. In the meantime, she would continue as before, teaching her charges and avoiding Lord Carnhaven whenever possible.

To avoid the earl, she made a point of visiting the library when he was out with his steward, or late at night when the house had gone to bed. The remainder of her time, she stayed in the school room, or with the girls.

"Can we go to the library?" Cassandra asked one afternoon.

"You finished the book you got yesterday?" Emma asked.

"No. It's very good, though. I just want to work on my assignment."

"Of course we can, Lady Cassandra. I'm very glad that you're enjoying your book, though."

A smile lit Cassandra's face. "I'm learning to read almost as well as Felicity, aren't I?"

"Yes, you are," Emma answered. "We shall visit the library after lunch with your father."

She saw the pleased expression on Cassandra's face and couldn't help but smile. Her charges were making remarkable progress, and joining their father for at least two meals a week had improved their table manners, as well as their ability to keep a conversation going.

The girls loved spending time with their father. Emma was the only one who found spending mealtime with Lord Carnhaven difficult.

Without seeming to realize what he was doing, he watched her with an intensity she found disturbing. Even more embarrassing were the times he caught her watching him in return.

She tried to ignore him, though she couldn't help but keep her gaze focused on his every move. There was a strength about everything he did, from the way he cut his meat, to how he held his glass, to the manner in which he put his napkin to his mouth that intrigued her. Instead of being soft and mannerly, each movement was a brisk, calculated exercise meant to accomplish a strategic purpose.

Their luncheons and dinnertimes were pure torture, but no matter how eager she was for them to end, she dreaded the time she would have to be parted from him. Emma scolded herself for such flighty behavior. She'd never felt this way about a man before. Especially a man who frightened her at the same time he excited her.

"Did you say we could visit the library now, Miss Sullivan?" Cassandra asked when their meal was over.

"I did," Emma answered as they rose from the table. "Do you wish to join us, my lord?"

"Uh, no," Spencer replied. "I have a meeting with my steward. Otherwise, I would be glad to go with you to see which books my daughters choose."

"I'm going to look for *Little Goody Two-Shoes*," Cassandra said.

"Why would you choose that?" her father asked. He smiled to try and cover his critical tone. "You've read it before. Several times."

"But that's the point, Papa. Miss Sullivan has assigned me a project to write a short epilogue to a story I know very well. I love how the wealthy man gave the little girl a pair of shoes that changed her life."

Lord Carnhaven looked suitably appreciative.

"And what about you, Felicity?" he asked.

"Oh I have plenty of books at the moment, Papa. My assignment now is to find three titles that I can link into one title as a theme for an entirely new story."

Carnhaven looked at his youngest daughter and smiled. "Well now. I shall want to be sure to hear what you come up with, Felicity."

The child beamed.

"Papa, did Miss Sullivan speak to you about teaching me to fish?"

Emma watched as the expression on Carnhaven's face darkened. The frustration she saw was similar to the anger she'd witnessed several nights earlier. It seemed clear now that it would never be possible for him to return to the site of the family's great tragedy.

"Come, ladies," she said, rising from the table and prompting her charges to hurry. She wanted to remove the girls from the room before they realized how upset their father was.

She led them to the library, and soon they were occupied with the books.

The more Emma thought on Lord Carnhaven's reaction to Felicity's question, the more determined she was to find a way around it.

⋙⋘

IT WAS BEAUTIFUL weather for her half-day, and Emma decided to walk to Isaac and Janey's. She'd written Janey earlier in the week informing her that she would come to call. Her friend was waiting for her when she arrived.

"Emma," Janey said, giving her a warm hug. "I've missed you terribly."

"I've missed you too. How are you? Is everything well with you?"

"Everything is more than well. It's perfect. I couldn't be happier."

Emma gave her friend another hug, then followed as she led the way to the morning room.

"Help me arrange these flowers while we talk," Janey said. "You're so good at it." She set an overflowing basket from the garden between them and the two fell, as always, into easy conversation as they worked. "How are you faring with your new charges?" she asked, which prompted Emma to go into a long explanation of how impressed she was with Cassandra and Felicity. She had just launched into the retelling of a particularly humorous escapade when the door opened and Isaac joined them.

"I'm so glad you came to call on my wife, Emma," he said, sitting down beside Janey and giving her a kiss on the cheek. "She's missed your company terribly."

"Isaac's correct," Janey said, reaching for Emma's hand and squeezing her fingers. "I *have* missed you."

"And I've missed *you*."

The three friends chatted for several more minutes, then the time was right for Emma to ask the question that had been plaguing her.

"You've known Lord Carnhaven for quite some time, haven't you, Isaac?"

"Yes. He was the first person I met when I moved to Willowbrook, and we became instant friends."

"Was his first wife still alive when you met?"

"Yes, she was. Why do you ask?"

"No reason. I just wondered what kind of person she was."

"She was, of course, one of the most beautiful women in the county," Isaac replied. "Felicity is an exact copy of her. Everything about her is the same as her mother."

"So you were a friend of theirs when she died."

"Oh, that was so tragic," Isaac said in an emotional voice. "Caroline loved the water. It was almost an obsession. She loved to spend time at the lake. She had taken her two daughters with her on a boat ride, as she often did. Spencer came upon them, and in her excitement at seeing him, she stood too quickly and capsized the boat. The servant rowing the boat saved Cassandra then went back for the nursemaid. Spencer swam out and reached baby Felicity and saved her, but could not return to save Caroline before she drowned."

"Oh my," Janey said, feeling the sting of tears. "How dreadfully sad."

Emma watched Janey reach for Isaac's hand to comfort him. "You said obsession. That she had almost an obsession about the water. Is that something she and Lord Carnhaven shared?"

Isaac shook his head and laughed softly. "Oh no, not at all. In fact, when they married, Caroline wouldn't go near the water. He spent weeks getting her over her fear of it. But once he got her into a boat, she couldn't get enough of it. She was obsessed, all right. We used to tease her about it."

Emma clasped her hands over her mouth. That explained so much. Of course he would blame himself for his wife's death. He'd turned her fear of water into an obsession with the lake. Of course he wouldn't introduce Felicity to the lake. She might love it. Might become obsessed with it herself. Might—

"May I ask why you inquired about Caroline's death, Emma?" Isaac asked.

"I asked because Felicity wanted to know if her father would teach her how to fish."

"Oh," Isaac said with a sigh. "I can guess at his reply."

"Yes, he became quite angry and forbade me from bringing up the subject ever again. He also forbade me from taking the girls anywhere near the lake. Now, of course, I understand."

"Yes," Isaac said. "He could never grant permission for such a thing. It's taken him a long time to recover from Caroline's death. In fact, I'm not sure he truly has."

"I'm quite sure he hasn't," Emma agreed.

Emma changed the subject without saying more. She would have to spend a great deal of time contemplating what course of action she should take next. She wasn't sure she should let the matter drop entirely. To forbid his daughters from experiencing the peacefulness of an afternoon at the lake would deprive them of that joy. And it certainly wouldn't help Lord Carnhaven heal from the tragedy of losing his wife.

This would take a great deal of thought.

Emma chatted with the couple a while longer, then Isaac offered to walk her to the door when it was time to leave.

"I debated whether or not to show you this," he said, removing an article from the pocket of his jacket, "but I think you need to see it, Emma."

"What is it?"

"It's from one of the scandal sheets Janey is so fond of reading."

Emma took the paper and looked at the article Isaac had left folded to the front. She read the first few words and felt the color drain from her face.

Authorities were notified again of a complaint issued against a certain Viscount S for attacking one of his mother's staff. This author wonders when someone will put a stop to this miscreant's evil actions. Soon, we hope.

Emma's head spun, but thankfully, Isaac was there to steady

her.

"Has Janey seen this?"

Isaac shook his head.

"Good. Don't let her see it."

"I won't. What are you going to do, Emma?"

"I don't know," she answered. "I know I can't stay here, though."

"Talk to Spence before you do anything, Emma. He'll know what's best."

Emma smiled at her friend. She might. Or she might not. She already knew what his answer would be, and she knew it was something she could not do.

Chapter Ten

Emma hadn't seen the Earl of Carnhaven for several days. He didn't join them for the meal they usually ate together, nor did she see him when he customarily met with his steward. Late on the third day, a footman delivered a missive informing Emma that her employer would be gone for several more days.

She wasn't sure where he'd gone, but it didn't really matter. She was sure he'd disappeared to avoid her and his daughters. Felicity was still more than a little piqued with him for getting angry with her for wanting to learn to fish.

Emma spent the time she had with the girls keeping them busy with schoolwork. She also took them for long walks every day when the weather cooperated. She may have been ordered to stay away from the lake, but that didn't mean they couldn't at least walk close enough to get a view of it.

"Oh," Cassandra said upon seeing the lake. "I didn't even know this was here. It's beautiful."

"Why do you think Father never brings us here?" Felicity asked.

"I don't know," Emma answered. "And perhaps you shouldn't tell him we've seen it. There must be a reason he doesn't want you to come here if he's never told you about it. I had forgotten that he warned me not to go near it." Even as she spoke the words, Emma hoped they would someday forgive her small lie.

"Then let's just make sure he doesn't find out we came here," Cassandra said.

Suddenly, Emma regretted her decision to take this particular path. She'd been given specific instructions not to go near the water. Instead, she was encouraging Carnhaven's daughters to keep something from their father. That went against everything she believed in.

"Perhaps we shouldn't have come this way," she said, overwhelmed with guilt. "I shouldn't have shown you the lake."

"Why not?" Felicity asked.

"Because your father didn't want you to come here, and I brought you anyway. We need to return home."

"But we've only walked a little way," Cassandra said. "I don't want to go back yet."

"I know you don't," Emma said. "But I'm afraid your father will consider my bringing you here a grave error in judgment. He expressly forbade it."

"Don't worry, Miss Sullivan," Felicity said as they turned back the way they'd come. "He'll never find out. We won't tell him, will we, Cassie?"

"Never," Cassandra said.

"Thank you, ladies. I appreciate your cooperation. We'll go back to the house, and if you would still like to walk some more, we'll take a turn around the garden. I'm sure the nice, warm weather has caused even more flowers to bloom."

"Do you think the rhododendrons might have blossomed?" Cassandra asked.

"I think it's likely. We'll go see."

The girls turned away from the lake and made their way along the path toward the house.

"Do you know where Father went?" Cassandra asked. "He's usually never gone this long."

"I heard him tell Jasper he had some business to take care of in London," Felicity said as they entered the house and made their way to the French doors that led to the garden.

Emma's blood ran cold. What if Carnhaven went to London for information concerning Slushman? What if he returned with news that the viscount was looking for her? That would force her to move faster than she intended.

She clutched her stomach, suddenly fearing she might be ill. She needed to sit down. She scanned the area ahead of her, and, seeing a bench along the side of the path, she rushed toward it.

"Are you all right, Miss Sullivan?" Cassandra asked when she and Felicity caught up with her.

Emma took one deep breath, then another. "Yes, I'm fine. I think I might have taken a little too much sun."

Cassandra and Felicity shared a confused look. The sun had stayed behind a cloud most of the afternoon, so they both knew that could not be the reason.

Cassie gave Emma a questioning look. "Does it bother you that Father isn't here, Miss Sullivan? Do you not feel safe when he's gone?"

Emma feigned a laugh. If only they knew that she would be much more in danger when he returned. "No, of course not. I feel safe at Carnhaven whether he is here or not."

"Good," Felicity said. "You should. Papa said Carnhaven is the safest place you can ever be."

"Yes, and your father is correct. Now, should we continue our walk?"

Emma rose and beckoned the girls onward.

IT HAD TAKEN Spencer much longer in London than he thought it would. At first, none of the acquaintances he thought to talk to were still in the city. They'd all gone to a house party in the country and weren't expected back until the following week. Finally, though, one or two of his closest friends returned, and he had a chance to meet with them in private.

"Carnhaven," the Earl of Marsten greeted him when Spencer entered the club he and most of his friends frequented. Marsten sat at a table with three university friends he and Spencer shared in common. "Come join us," Marsten said, and called for another bottle of brandy and a glass for Spencer.

"What brings you to London?" a second friend asked.

"Estate business," Spencer replied after he filled his glass and took a swallow. "It seems there is never an end to it."

"Same with me, old boy," the Marquess of Revelow added. "I didn't know how carefree my life was before my father died. Nor did I realize how much of the running of the estate he handled."

Spencer listened as his friends relived their carefree school days, then brought up the topic he wanted to discuss. "I heard a rumor that Earl Pearlman's son was badly injured in an accident. Did he survive?"

"As a matter of fact, he did," Marsten answered, "but it was no accident. Someone tried to kill him. Stabbed him with a letter opener, as I recall."

"Did they ever find the footpads who did it?" Spencer asked.

"No," Revelow replied. "Except it wasn't any footpad who did it. It was either one of the upstairs maids or the earl's governess. They both disappeared that night."

"Have they been found?"

"No," Marsten said, "but it's not for lack of searching. Pearlman is bloody bent on finding them."

The friends grunted their distaste. "Wait a moment," a third friend said as he leaned forward to hush the group. "Pearlman wants the subject dropped. It's that damned lout of a son who's so desperate to find them and see them hanged. Everyone knows Slushman is a no-good reprobate. He's left a string of bastards all over the East End. Every one of them has Slushman's red hair and blue eyes."

Marsten added to the tale. "He takes advantage of the lass, and when she turns up pregnant, he gives her the boot. After she's gone, he doesn't provide for a one of them."

"So he's the one who wants them found," Spencer said.

"Yes, he has runners looking everywhere for them. It's only a matter of time before they're found," Revelow replied. "Is there a reason you are interested?"

Spencer shook his head. "No, I just overheard some acquaintances talking about this."

"Well, whoever stabbed him did a fine job of it. Slushman nearly died, and he isn't going to let his assailant get away without paying for what she did to him."

Spencer changed the subject as quickly as possible and talked about the latest Society scandals. But he couldn't forget what he'd learned from his friends.

Emma had been correct to assume Slushman would come after her. That was exactly what the dog intended. Spencer knew now that he should have believed her. She truly wasn't safe until Slushman was locked away.

SPENCER LEFT HIS friends and made the decision to leave London yet that night. He knew it would be late by the time he returned home, but he was in a hurry to get there. He needed to make sure Emma was safe. Thinking of her prediction of what Slushman might do if he were still alive was frightening enough. But hearing what Spencer's trusted friends had to say was several times more terrifying.

Spencer pushed his horse as fast as he dared. It wasn't safe to go too fast because of the darkness, but the closer he got, the more impatient he was to get home.

Surely Emma was safe, or Jasper would have sent for him. He wasn't as worried that something had happened to Emma as he was that she had decided again that no one was safe as long as she was there and had run away.

Spencer finally arrived home. He dismounted and handed the reins to a stable hand who came running half-dressed and still half-asleep.

Jasper stood with the door open and greeted Spencer as he entered.

"Oh, my lord. I'm ever so glad to see you."

Spencer handed his butler his coat, hat, and gloves. "Has something happened? Is everything all right, Jasper?"

There was a slight hesitation before Jasper answered. "It's Miss Sullivan, my lord."

Spencer had never seen the butler so agitated. "What it is it, Jasper? What is wrong with Miss Sullivan?"

"I think perhaps she might be ill."

"What makes you think that?"

"She hasn't slept since you left for London. I hear her up at all hours, and she roams the whole house from the time she gets the girls to bed until the next morning. And she hasn't eaten enough to keep a bird alive."

"Thank you, Jasper. Perhaps I'll stop in to see her before I retire."

"You won't find her in her room, my lord. I believe she's in the library."

"Thank you, Jasper. You may go to bed now. I'll lock up."

"Yes, my lord."

Spencer walked to the library door and took a deep breath before he rapped softly and entered. Emma must not have heard him, for she stood at the French doors that led to the terrace with her arms wrapped around her tightly in a very protective manner.

"Emma?"

She heard him and turned. Spencer's heart broke.

Streaks of wetness ran down her cheeks, and her eyes were red and puffy. The fear she was experiencing was evident on her face. She was terrified.

Spencer took several steps toward her until he was so close to her he could reach out and pull her to him. He couldn't stop himself. He needed to hold her. He needed to have her in his arms. He needed to keep her close and show her he was here for her.

He wasn't sure what her reaction would be. He hoped she wouldn't turn away from him. He prayed she would let him hold her, to show her in the only way he could that he cared for her. That he more than cared for her.

He held out his arms and, with a soft cry, she stepped into his embrace.

"He's still alive," she said.

Her words weren't loud and demanding, but soft and timid, as if she feared his answer.

"Yes. He's still alive," Spencer whispered. "And he's determined to find you."

He felt her answer with a nod of her head against his chest.

"Very well," she said. "Then I know what I have to do. I will be gone in the morning."

"You will *not* be gone in the morning. You are never going anywhere. You won't be safe if you leave, and you know it."

"But I can't stay here. You will not be safe. Your daughters will not be safe."

"I will be safe, and my daughters will be safe. And, if you trust me, you will be safe too."

Emma shook her head. "You don't know what he's like, my lord. He's—"

"I heard enough about him while in London that I know the world would be a better place if you had killed him."

She lifted her head from his chest, and their gazes locked. A feeling came over him like he hadn't experienced since Caroline died. A feeling of completeness. The need to have someone to hold and care for, to take care *of*.

He'd gone without fulfilling this need for so long that he feared he might die if he didn't satisfy this desire.

"Emma?" he whispered.

"My lord?"

"Spencer. Just Spencer, please."

The look on her face was a mixture of confusion and desire. But even more, of want and need. And Spencer had no choice but to answer that need.

He lowered his head and pressed his lips to hers.

He experienced a hunger he hadn't felt for a long time, for years. It was the first time he'd kissed Emma since that fragile moment in the gazebo. That had been a parting kiss, a kiss of goodbye. This was different in so many ways. This time he let passion rule. And with wonder, he sensed this may have been the first time Emma had kissed any man.

He wrapped his arms around her in a possessive manner and deepened his kiss. He reminded himself not to overwhelm, not to rush Emma, and yet her response was not telling him to slow down, but to offer more.

He relished the cloak of darkness. It gave him courage. Spencer tilted her head to gain better access and kissed her again, deeply. He didn't want to stop, and clearly, neither did she. Emma entwined her fingers in his hair and kept his lips locked to hers, allowing him to consume more of her. And he did.

EMMA LET HERSELF sink into his embrace. She'd sensed from the moment they'd met that Spencer Washburn, Earl of Carnhaven, may well be the only man she could ever love. He was the only man she'd ever been drawn to with such ferocity. The only man who'd ever intrigued her as he did. Yet she knew he was the one man she could never have. The one man she could destroy. The one man whose association with her might get them *both* killed.

Emma kissed him one last time, then broke their kiss and buried her head against his chest. It was several moments before either of them could speak.

The comfort and security she experienced when he held her

almost allowed her to believe that he *could* keep her safe. Would that it were true, but that was only possible if she allowed herself to forget how evil Slushman was. Forgetting the depth of Slushman's malevolence would get anyone she cared for killed.

"Are you all right?" Carnhaven asked.

"Yes, I'm fine. I must apologize, though."

"Don't you dare."

The surprise on his face was easy to read. He honestly considered *himself* at fault for kissing her.

Emma stepped out of his arms and seated herself on the sofa nearest them. He walked to the liquor cart and filled two glasses with wine.

"Here," he said, handing her one of the glasses.

When she took it, he sat beside her and reached for her hand. He sensed she needed the contact as she explained what she'd decided to do if she discovered Slushman was still alive and intended to come after her.

"I know what you're thinking, Emma. You're trying to decide if you're going to tell me you're leaving, or if you're just going to let us figure it out when we wake in the morning to find you gone. Am I correct?"

Emma tried to pull her hand out of his grasp, but he would not release her fingers.

"Please, my lord—"

"Spencer."

"Yes. Spencer. You know I can't stay, and you know the reason why. I can't let Slushman know I'm here. Or even that I *was* here and that I've grown fond of you and your daughters. He's not averse to taking his hatred out on you, or even Cassandra and Felicity, simply because you've been kind to me."

"Where will you go?"

"I don't know. Further away from London. Perhaps to America."

Spencer drew her closer. "I'm not sure I can let you go, Emma. I feel that I've just found you. I can't lose you now."

She brought her hands up and cupped Spencer's cheeks, then brought his mouth down to meet hers. She kissed him with all the passion she felt for him, then rested her forehead against his.

She loved him. She knew she did, and letting him go would be the hardest thing she'd ever have to do.

"Do something for me," he whispered in her ear.

"If I can," she answered.

"Give me a week before you leave. Stay with me at least that long."

Something told Emma that was too long to stay, but she had no excuse for denying him. "I… I…"

"Please."

She did trust him. If there was anyone in the world who might protect her from danger, it was him. Did she dare stay?

Emma released the breath that had been imprisoned too long within her. "Very well," she whispered.

"Thank you," he replied in a hushed tone as he lowered his head and kissed her again. This time the touch of his lips was demanding, intense, communicating a passion that she welcomed with her whole heart.

When they finally drew apart, Spencer refused to release her. Instead, he held her close.

"I don't think I'll ever be able to let you go, Emma. I need you too desperately."

She clung to him with greedy desperation. "You have to, Spencer. Neither you nor your daughters will be safe as long as I'm here. You'd never forgive yourself if something happened to them because of me. Nor could I forgive myself. Now," she said, and released him, "I need to get to bed, and so do you."

He stole one more kiss, then walked with her to the door. The moment she left him, she wished she hadn't promised him a week. That was reckless, and she was afraid she would regret having made such a promise.

Chapter Eleven

For the next few days, Carnhaven left every morning early and didn't return until late in the afternoon. Emma would ask him where he'd gone, but he'd avoid giving her any specifics. The only thing she would notice was that when he returned, several men she'd never seen before would be taking up positions around the estate. And the men all carried weapons.

Isaac and Janey also came to call on her every day. They usually arrived around teatime. Janey and Emma and the girls would enjoy tea and pastries, and Isaac would join Spencer in his study. By the end of the week that she had promised him, Emma was a nervous wreck.

Several things were obvious. The first was that Spencer had no intention of letting her leave. He intended to confine her to Carnhaven Manor. The second thing she realized was that the added men he'd hired were not there just to guard his daughters. They were there to guard *her*.

"How long do you intend to pretend that you have everything under control, Spencer?" she asked one day. "We can't live like this much longer. Even your daughters are tired of being locked in."

He stood and walked from behind his desk to take her in his arms. "You're not locked in, Emma. You can leave the house any time you want. You just cannot go out the front, nor can you go out alone."

"I can't remain here, Spencer. That was our agreement. I said I would stay here one week, then leave. My week is up tomorrow."

"I changed our agreement, Emma. I can't let you leave tomorrow. You won't be safe."

"I can't stay here. *You* won't be safe."

"Sit with me," he said, leading her to the sofa and sitting beside her.

Emma summoned her sternest voice. "For one second, imagine what might happen if Slushman finds me. Imagine what he'll do to anyone who tries to stop him from getting to me."

"I have enough guards to protect you that he won't be able to touch you."

"And when he realizes I'm that well protected, what do you think he'll do?" When he didn't answer her, she repeated her question. "What do you think he'll do, Spencer? Would you like to tell me, or do you want me to tell you?"

When he still didn't answer, Emma rose to her feet. "He'll hire an army of men to kill the men you hired to protect me. That's what he'll do, and you know it. Some of them will die. Because of me. Because I'm here."

"It won't get to that point," Spencer said.

"Ha!" Emma replied. "Even one innocent man dying is too many. I'm not worth it."

Spencer shot to his feet and clasped her upper arms. "Don't you ever say that. You are worth a thousand Slushmans."

When Emma didn't say anything in return, he wrapped his arms around her and pulled her close.

"Oh, sweetheart. I didn't mean to sound so gruff. I know what you're going through, and I know how difficult this is for you. But it will be over soon, and we won't ever have to think about Slushman again."

"Do you think so, Spencer?" she asked, tucking her head beneath his chin and nestling close to him.

"I know so," he answered, but Emma heard the rapid beating of his heart, and it belied the confidence she heard in his voice.

The man she'd fallen in love with was afraid for her. For probably the first time in his life, there was an evil force out there he wasn't sure he could defeat—at least not before it destroyed someone Spencer loved.

Emma lifted her head and studied the man she'd fallen in love with. Her heart ached with the affection she felt. She tried to memorize his every feature, from the high arches of his cheekbones, to the chiseled cut of his jaw, to the perfect lines of his brows and nose. He was as perfect as any man she'd ever seen. Every part of him emitted strength and power. She couldn't find anything to fault. He was perfect in every way.

"What are you going to do now, Spencer?"

He took her back to the sofa and sat with her. He kept her close to him and wrapped her in his arms.

"I'm going to have to go to London and talk to Scotland Yard. I need to know what they intend to do about him and what lengths I may go to if he should come after you."

Emma nodded. In her mind, that was a logical move. The last thing she wanted was for Spencer to get into trouble for handling Slushman the wrong way. "When are you leaving?"

"In the morning. The sooner I know what I can and cannot do, the faster we can get this over with. But I need you to promise me that you will stay here until I return. I can't spend my time worrying about you, Emma."

"I'll be here when you return," she promised. "The girls and I won't go anywhere except the garden."

"That's my girl. I'll be back as soon as I can."

"I know you will," she said, and snuggled closer to him.

He was leaving again. That was good. All she needed was a couple of hours to get her things together.

SPENCER WAS GONE the next morning before Emma rose. When her charges were dressed for the day, she took them down for breakfast. After they finished, she couldn't bring herself to pretend this was a usual day. This was her last day with Lady Cassandra and Felicity. She didn't want to spend it in the classroom. Instead, she wanted to spend it as a free day, one the girls would remember enjoying with her.

"This day is entirely too pleasant to spend indoors," she said when they were prepared to leave the dining room. "I've decided we are not going to spend it in the classroom."

"What are we going to do?" Felicity said with excitement.

"We are going outdoors. We are going to take a stroll in the garden, then sit in the gazebo and read."

"Oh," Cassandra said with a smile lighting her face. "May I read my Jane Austen book aloud? I'm at a very exciting part, and I can't wait to see what happens."

"That sounds perfect," Emma said. "Run to your room and get your book, and we'll wait for you."

Cassandra ran upstairs for her book and came right back down.

"On an ordinary day, I'm afraid I'd have to reprimand you for the way you ran up and down the stairs," Emma chided her. "A lady never runs as you just did. That was not at all dignified."

"Sorry, Miss Sullivan," Cassie said. "I was just in such a hurry that—"

"There's no need for excuses, Lady Cassandra. An apology will suffice."

"Yes, Miss Sullivan."

"Very well," Emma said. "Now, let's take that stroll through the garden so we can settle in the gazebo and you can read to us, my lady."

Cassie and Felicity looped their arms through each other's and strolled along the path. Emma tried to keep the tears from filling her eyes but lost her battle. Oh, she would miss her girls. She'd never grown so close to any of her charges as she had to

Spencer Carnhaven's daughters. They were more special than any children she'd ever worked with. Their love for her was an unexpected reward that she deeply treasured.

When they reached the gazebo, the girls took the two steps up and sat on the bench that lined the perimeter. Emma sat close to them.

"Are you crying, Miss Sullivan?" Felicity asked in surprise when they were all seated.

"I'm not crying," Emma said, wiping the wetness from her cheeks. "I was just thinking how fast you ladies are growing, and how soon you will have your come-outs and meet the men of your dreams."

The two girls looked at each other and giggled. "Don't worry, Miss Sullivan. You aren't going to get rid of us that soon. We're only eight and ten," Cassandra said with rosy cheeks.

"Yes," Emma said with a lump in her throat. "And this is how I'll always remember you. Now, Cassandra. Would you like to read to us?"

"I'd love to, Miss Sullivan."

Emma listened to Cassandra's lilting voice and promised herself that each night when she went to bed, she would remember the sound and it would speak to her of what she left behind.

Emma was woolgathering when a frantic yell brought her back from her daydreams. She bolted upright and realized that Jasper was calling to her.

"Run, Miss Sullivan! Run!"

Emma turned, and her breath caught in her throat. Six men raced ahead of Jasper. She didn't recognize five of the men, but they carried the unmistakable look of Scotland Yard. Unfortunately, she did recognize the sixth man.

Emma focused on the man's bright red hair above his startling blue eyes, and her blood ran cold.

Slushman.

His glare locked on her with more hatred than she'd ever

seen in anyone's eyes.

She whirled around to face Cassie and Felicity. "You need to get away from here. Run to the house as fast as you can. To the back, past the kitchen garden! Jasper will help you. Now, go!"

Emma pushed the girls from the gazebo and watched them run toward the house. Jasper caught up with them and wrapped an arm around each one to hurry them to safety.

Emma turned to confront the men and was shocked to see Lord Slushman so close to her that he could touch her. Except he didn't touch her. He clenched his hand in a fist and hit her so hard the sunlight disappeared for a moment.

"Slushman! That's enough," a second man bellowed, taking a step toward the viscount.

Unfortunately, the man didn't reach Slushman before he pulled his arm back and hit her again. This blow was harder than the last, and the sun faded for longer.

"I said, *enough*!" the man bellowed. He obviously outranked the other men. He stepped up beside Emma and held her steady so she didn't lose her balance. "You're safe now, Miss Sullivan. I'm an agent from Scotland Yard. I'm afraid we must take you to London with us. The inspector would like to ask you a few questions, and we... We'll have a doctor see to you."

"I don't know why you're worried about the bitch," Slushman growled. "It won't be long and she'll be swinging from a rope."

"If you had a brain in your head, my lord, you would know I've taken as much from you as I intend to take, and if you don't want to end up in a cell yourself, you'll shut your trap."

"You can't—"

"I can. And I will!"

Just then, at least a half dozen of the men Spencer had hired to protect them arrived with their guns drawn. The men from Scotland Yard drew their weapons and prepared to fire on them.

"No!" Emma yelled. "Don't! I'll go with you."

The men lowered their weapons, all except Slushman. The

agent from Scotland Yard walked to him and took the pistol out of his hand. Slushman glared at him, but let him keep it.

"Come with me," the agent said, wrapping his arm around Emma's shoulder. She was thankful. She wasn't sure she would have made it to the house on her own.

The agent escorted her to the house to let Cook tend to her wounds, and a short time later was hurrying her out the front door. Jasper held the door, and she paused before she left the house. "Take care of Lord Carnhaven's daughters, Jasper. I'm sure he will be back soon. Tell him I am all right."

Emma didn't wait for a response before she stepped into the carriage with the very recognizable crest of Scotland Yard emblazoned on its door. Thankfully, the agent followed her into the carriage and the door closed, leaving Slushman outside to ride behind them.

"I am Agent Williams, Miss Sullivan. I apologize for the way Slushman accosted you."

"That's not your fault, Agent Williams. He's a cruel man of whom I would expect no less."

"What are you going to do now?"

Emma thought for several long minutes. Finally she answered, "I don't know." And she honestly didn't.

SPENCER PUSHED HIS horse to arrive home as quickly as possible. When he finally approached the house, he dismounted and handed the reins to a stable hand who came running to him. Jasper stood with the door open, and Spencer could tell by one look at him that something was terribly wrong.

"What's wrong, Jasper. What's happened?" Spencer had never seen his butler so agitated.

"It's Miss Sullivan! Several men came earlier. Some of them were from Scotland Yard. She's been arrested. They took her to

London."

Spencer's heart plummeted to the pit of his stomach. "Was there a man with red hair with them?"

"Yes, my lord. Bright red hair."

Spencer clutched his hands into fists at his sides. He'd never been so furious—or so frightened—in his life. He didn't know what would happen to her. He didn't know what Slushman would do to her, or if she would even make it to London.

"Where are the girls?"

"They're both in Felicity's room."

"Were they with Miss Sullivan when the men came?"

"Yes, my lord. They're extremely upset. The man with the red hair attacked Miss Sullivan. He struck her. More than once."

"Damn!" Spencer yelled, then took off at a run. He needed to get to his daughters and assure them that everything would be all right—even if he wasn't sure it would be.

He raced up the stairs to Felicity's room. He knew that was where Cassandra would go. She always went to Felicity for comfort.

He opened the door and found them on the bed wrapped in each other's arms.

"Papa!" they cried out when they saw him. They leaped from the bed and raced to him. When they reached him, they wrapped their arms around him and held on as if to never let him go. "Some men took Miss Sullivan away," they cried out in unison.

"Hush, my darlings. I've got you now. You're safe."

Spencer tried to comfort them, but they were so distraught that it was difficult to calm them.

"Felicity, tell me what happened." He knew that Felicity would be less dramatic than Cassandra, and more factual, so he asked her to explain what the men had said.

"Oh, Papa! It was terrible. As soon as the men came toward us, Miss Sullivan tried to protect us, but the man with the red hair jerked her away from us. He hit her twice before the man from Scotland Yard stopped him."

"Did he hurt her?"

"She was bleeding, but Cook helped bind up the wound before they left."

Spencer was raging mad. So help him, if Slushman hurt her any further, he'd kill him.

"Papa, you'll go after Miss Sullivan and bring her back, won't you?" Felicity asked.

"Yes, sweethearts. I'll find her and bring her home. This is where she belongs." He hugged both his daughters and gave them kisses. "You go to sleep now. I'll be back with Miss Sullivan before you know it."

Spencer tucked his daughters back into bed, then pulled the covers over them and left their room.

"Jasper, have my valet pack enough clothes for several days and follow me to London. I'll be at the townhouse."

"Yes, my lord. Are you leaving tonight?"

"Yes. I can't bear the thought of Emma sleeping in a filthy cell any longer than necessary."

Spencer grabbed his cloak, hat, and gloves and went outside. One of the stable hands had fresh horses hooked to the carriage, and he sped away toward London. He was serious when he said he couldn't stand to think of Emma sleeping in a filthy cell for even an hour, let alone all night.

CHAPTER TWELVE

SPENCER STOPPED AT Isaac's on his way to London and told him what had transpired. Janey, of course, overheard them talking and dissolved into tears. She blamed herself for Emma having been arrested, and no matter how much the men tried to convince her that none of this was her fault, it didn't help. She blamed herself.

Spencer left, and Isaac promised he'd be right behind him. Spencer knew his friend wouldn't allow him to go through this alone, and he was thankful. Isaac's legal expertise would be invaluable.

He went straight to Scotland Yard and talked to the man in charge of Emma's case, an Inspector Whitaker.

"Follow me," Whitaker said, and led Spencer to an inner office where they could speak in private. "Would you care for something to drink?" he asked when Spencer was seated. "Whiskey, perhaps?"

"I'd appreciate that," Spencer said gratefully. He accepted the whiskey Whitaker offered and took a swallow. "Where do you have Miss Sullivan?"

"She's in a cell. Slushman insisted that she was a dangerous criminal."

"There's nothing dangerous about her. She's governess to my two daughters."

The inspector walked to the window. "I'd like to speak to you off the record. Do I have your word that what I tell you will be kept in the strictest confidence?"

Spencer nodded, and the inspector opened a drawer on the side of his desk and removed a thick folder. "This contains the complaints we've received on Lord Slushman over the last few years. They are all assault and rape charges. All filed by female staff members who worked for Slushman's parents."

Spencer reached for the file and skimmed through it. "This is terrifying," he said, reading one rape charge after another. "How can you stop him?"

"We can't. He commits all these crimes inside his parents' home. As soon as one of the victims complains, he denies anything happened. We can't prove that he attacked a maid, and, of course, who is going to take the word of an uneducated servant over that of a peer of the realm?"

"I see. Do you have any suggestions as to how we can prove his guilt?"

"Not yet, but we can't let him get by raping more innocent young girls."

"And I refuse to let him get by with harming one of my employees. He has to be stopped. May I take this folder with me?"

The inspector shook his head. "I'm sorry, I can't let the folder leave Scotland Yard. But, for further reference, I have included the names, addresses, and dates of the attacks inside, if that can be used in…in any way."

Spencer tried to imagine what the inspector was telling him.

"Now, I take it you'd like to see Miss Sullivan?"

"Yes, I would."

"I'll get someone to show you to her cell, but I warn you, Lord Slushman was not gentle in his treatment of her, at least not until my agent stopped him. If his treatment of Miss Sullivan is an example of his true character, he needs to be locked up and the key thrown away."

Whitaker turned to the door as if he intended to leave. "I'll be right back," he said. But first he flipped open the folder. Lying on top was a list of all the females Slushman had raped and the dates they had leveled a charge against him.

Spencer took the paper, folded it, and slid it into his pocket, then placed the cover back over the folder. He made sure everything was back in place before Whitaker returned, and left without a word.

SPENCER FOLLOWED THE guard down a flight of stairs, then down a long, dark hallway. The guard slowed when he neared a cell, then unlocked and opened it. Spencer took a deep breath before he entered the cell.

He knew Emma had to have heard him, but she did not turn around to face him. She stood with her arms wrapped around herself in a very protective manner.

"Emma?"

She heard him and turned. Spencer's heart broke.

Streaks of wetness ran down her cheeks, and her eyes were red and puffy. The fear she was experiencing was evident on her face. As were several dark bruises.

Spencer extended his arms toward her and took a step forward. Before he took a second step, she rushed forward and wrapped her arms around him.

"Emma," he said, kissing her face repeatedly.

"Spencer," she said, wrapping her arms around his neck.

"Are you all right?" he asked before kissing her again.

"I am now."

Emma tucked her head beneath Spencer's chin and pressed her cheek against his chest. He held her close as if he'd never have to let her go.

"What are we going to do now?" she asked.

"We're going to have to figure out how to defend you. We

have to paint Slushman in the worst light possible. The judge has to see what a worthless human being the man is, and that you feared for Janey's life and attacked him to save her."

"Can we do that?"

"We have to. We don't have a choice."

"Oh, Spencer, I'm so sorry I involved you in this. I'm not the kind of person you wanted your daughters to associate with."

He kissed the top of her head. "You are exactly the type of woman I want my daughters to emulate. You are exactly the person I want at my side."

"I love you, Spencer," she whispered, barely loud enough for him to hear.

"And I love you, Emma."

SPENCER STAYED WITH Emma as long as he could, then went back to talk to Inspector Whitaker. The police had more information than before, and none of it encouraging.

Viscount Slushman had been to see the inspector, wanting to make sure Emma was locked up securely and unable to escape, or have help escaping. Whitaker assured him he had no worries on that account, and if he continued to harass Scotland Yard, the simpering man would be locked in the cell across from Emma's and he could watch her himself to make sure she didn't escape.

Spencer almost found that humorous, but Whitaker's next bit of news removed any hint of that. The judge had been assigned to Emma's trial, and it was Horacio Longman, who was reputed to be the harshest magistrate in all of London.

"That wasn't the luckiest draw for a magistrate, my lord," Whitaker said. "One thing about him is that he may be harsh, but he is fair. Slushman won't be able to pay him off."

"That's good," Spencer agreed.

"Do you know how you're going to defend Miss Sullivan?"

"Not yet," Spencer said, "but I've got two days. The trial isn't until Monday."

"If there's anything I can do, let me know. I want Slushman locked away as much as you do."

"Thank you, Inspector," Spencer said, then left Whitaker's office. He stopped to see Emma once more for a short time, then went directly to his townhouse. When he arrived, he was thankful to see Isaac's carriage. Spencer needed someone to discuss strategy with. And two days wasn't a lot of time to come up with a foolproof plan to save her.

"I'm glad to see you," he said when he entered.

"Is Emma all right?" Janey asked, wiping the wetness from her eyes.

"She'll be much better when we get her out of that prison."

"This is all my fault, Spencer," she said through her tears.

Spencer clasped his hands around her arms. "No, Janey. This is not your fault. The only person who is responsible for what happened is Slushman."

"I know," Janey said, struggling to hold back the tears. "But Emma saved me. Slushman would have hurt me if she hadn't come to help me."

"That's the kind of person Emma is," Spencer said. "She would have done the same for anyone Slushman attacked."

"Do you have any ideas how we're going to save her?" Isaac asked.

"One or two. But I'm not sure they'll work."

Just then there was a knock on the door, and Spencer's butler came into the salon where they were gathered. "You have guests, my lord. They say they are friends of yours."

Spencer couldn't imagine who might be here. He didn't know anyone even knew he was in London.

"Show them in, Flowers."

"Yes, my lord."

Flowers left, then returned with three men following him.

"Marsten," Spencer greeted his friend. "Revelow. Paulson. I

didn't know anyone even knew I was in London."

"News travels quickly in our circles," Marsten replied. "We came to see if we could be of any help."

"I appreciate your offer. Let me introduce you."

Spencer introduced his friends to Isaac and Janey while Flowers filled glasses with brandy. Then they all sat.

"You said you had an idea how to help Emma," Isaac said.

"I do, but I'm not sure it will work."

"Let's hear it," Revelow said. "At least it's a starting point. There are six of us. Surely we can add enough to your idea to guarantee its success."

Spencer reached into his jacket pocket and removed the list he'd taken from Inspector Whitaker's file. "This is a list of women who have filed complaints against Slushman for raping them and getting them with child." He passed the list from one man gathered there to the next.

"Damn!"

"Bloody hell!"

"Damn!" one after another said when they saw the list.

"What's your idea, Carnhaven?" Marsten asked.

"Surely we can convince one of the women on this list to testify against Slushman."

"Will one be enough?" Marsten asked.

"It will have to be. I doubt we'll find more."

CHAPTER THIRTEEN

SPENCER SAT ON a stool next to Emma's cell and watched her sleep. He had come in the night, after his friends had formed a plan to prove what a reprobate Slushman was. He'd brought her a blanket and some bread and cheeses his cook had prepared. He could tell she'd been so worried that she hadn't eaten anything for some time.

"Have you been here all night?" she asked when she woke.

Spencer smiled. Oh, he loved her. Loved everything about her.

"I love watching you sleep. I can't wait until I can wake up every morning and watch you wake."

Her unguarded blush was followed by a frown furrowing her brow. "You know that may not happen, Spencer. If the magistrate finds me guilty, he may sentence me to hang."

"No, he won't, Emma. We'll prove that you're innocent. That you stabbed Slushman to protect Janey."

"But he may sentence me to life in prison."

"Stop it," he warned her. "He won't do that either."

Spencer reached for her hand and held it. When she looked at him, the first tears fell from her eyes.

"I'm frightened, Spencer."

"I know you are. I am too. But this will be over soon, and everything will be all right."

Spencer leaned his face through the bars and kissed Emma as thoroughly as he could. He pressed his lips to hers and showed her as best he could that he loved her.

"I have to leave now," he said, bringing her hands to his lips and kissing her fingers.

"Thank you, Spencer. For everything."

"You are welcome, sweetheart. Don't worry. This will be over soon, and you will be home with me and the girls."

Emma smiled at him, and the sad look almost broke his heart.

EMMA WATCHED SPENCER walk away from her, then listened until she could no longer hear his footsteps in the stone corridor. She never thought it was possible to find someone to love as much as she loved Spencer, Earl of Carnhaven. She never thought it was possible to fall in love as deeply as she had. But he was perfect. She couldn't have found anyone more perfect.

Janey came to sit with her in the afternoon and shared all the news she'd heard, including that several friends of Spencer's had come to help with the plan he and Isaac had formulated to prove that Emma's actions were justified.

In the evening, Spencer returned, but she sent him home. She knew he'd managed very little sleep the night before, and if he wanted to be alert enough to face the magistrate in the morning, he had to get a decent night's sleep. She finally convinced him she would be safe, and he left her.

The next morning, she woke early and prepared to face what might be the last day of her life. When Spencer arrived, she walked with him from the prison cell into the bright sunshine. Surely that was a good sign.

"Look at how beautiful today is," she said, looking up to the clear blue sky. "I think having the sunshine taken away for as long as I was in that cell made me realize how much I missed the sunlight."

Spencer wrapped his arm around her and held her closer. "After today, I promise we'll take a walk in the sunlight every day the weather allows."

Emma lifted her gaze until it locked with his. She smiled through the tears that swam in her eyes. "I love you, Spencer. No matter what happens today, never forget that."

"I won't, Emma. I know you do. As I love you."

He lifted her hand and pressed her palm to his chest so she could feel his heartbeat. She kept her gaze focused on him, memorizing every perfect feature of his face, from his high cheekbones to his strong, chiseled jaw, to the inky darkness of his expressive eyes. But more than his physical features, she wanted to remember his calm confidence and his captivating presence. Even though she couldn't convince herself that today would turn out for the best, she absorbed the confidence he emitted. All the strength that consumed her came from him. Spencer *was* her strength. Because of him, she would survive whatever happened today.

"WE'RE HERE," HE said as the paddy wagon slowed then came to a halt. "Are you ready?"

"Yes," she answered. "No matter what happens, it will be fine."

He leaned toward her and gave her a quick kiss, then exited the enclosed carriage and helped her descend. The guard who had ridden with them exited, and when Emma stepped out, she was surrounded by a small crowd of people. Some of them she knew, like Isaac and Janey, but many of them she had never seen before.

Janey stepped up to her and gave her a warm hug. "We're here for you, Emma."

"I know, Janey."

Her friend wiped her eyes. "This should be me having to answer for what happened that night."

"No, Janey. You went through enough."

"I'll never forget what you did for me. Never."

Before Emma had time to say more, Inspector Whitaker motioned for them to follow him.

"Hold on tight, Emma," Spencer said, "and don't look around."

"Is *he* here?"

"Yes, in all his gloating arrogance and haughtiness. Don't look at him."

Spencer led her inside the building. He stopped just after they entered and spoke to a man she didn't know. "Did we find at least one who would come?"

The man smiled. "Yes."

Spencer breathed a sigh of satisfaction. Inspector Whitaker led the way, and Spencer followed with Emma on his arm.

"Where is the jury?" she asked.

"There isn't one. This isn't a murder trial. The judge will rule the verdict."

"Oh," Emma said. "Is that good or bad?"

Spencer showed her to a chair. "I'll tell you when he hands down a ruling," he whispered, and sat in the chair next to her.

Emma nodded, then made the tragic error of turning her head and looking across the room. Her eyes locked on Lord Slushman, and a painful knot plummeted to the pit of her stomach.

The malicious look on his face was matched only by the evil glare in his eyes.

"Don't look at him, sweetheart," Spencer said. "He isn't worth getting upset over."

"You're correct."

"Of course I am," he teased, and Emma almost felt she could smile.

Before she could respond to Spencer, the judge who would

preside over her trial entered the courtroom.

Emma attempted to form an opinion about the kind of man who would determine her fate, but she found it impossible. He was a difficult man to read, other than she surmised he was a harsh taskmaster. He followed the law and did not excuse wrongdoing. This would work against her because of what she had done. But it would also work against Slushman if they could prove that he had taken advantage of several of Lady Pearlman's female staff.

She clutched her hands in her lap and tried to force herself to breathe.

The magistrate started the trial. He explained the charges that were brought against Emma by Viscount Slushman, then asked Slushman to elaborate on the charges.

The viscount stood and, with a great amount of pomposity, described the events of the night of the attack.

"Miss Sullivan was a member of my family's staff. She served as governess to my two sisters. There was no excuse for her unprovoked attack. I cannot imagine what possessed her to attack me so viciously. I had not previously spoken more than two words to her. Unless jealousy was the cause for her outburst."

"Please explain your last statement, Lord Slushman," the magistrate said. "How could you think jealousy played a part in the attack if you had never spoken to her?"

"Well, my lord, I have been told that I possess above-average looks and a certain charm and charisma."

The people in the gallery chuckled, and a few applauded his self-importance and conceit.

The magistrate pounded his gavel to quiet the crowd, and when the court was settled, he ordered Slushman to continue.

"Well, as I said, perhaps Miss Sullivan was jealous that I didn't pay as much attention to her as I did the other female staff members. It was usual for the female staff, especially the upstairs maids, to vie for my attention."

"But Miss Sullivan did not?"

"Oh, she tried," Slushman said with a snide glance in her direction. "But her type didn't interest me."

"I see. Go on."

"Well, on the night in question I was in conversation with one of the upstairs maids and, without provocation, Miss Sullivan came up behind me and stabbed me several times with a metal letter opener."

There was a loud gasp from the crowd, and Spencer placed his hand over her clenched fists and squeezed her fingers in support.

"Is there anything else you'd like to add?" the magistrate asked.

"Yes, your honor. The court needs to know that Miss Sullivan is a dangerous villain. If it hadn't been for my strong constitution and overwhelming will to live, I would have died from the wounds she inflicted. She is deranged, your honor. She's a vicious killer and needs to be removed from society."

There was a loud chorus of jeering and cries for Emma to be thrown into prison. Even a few calls for her to be hanged.

Emma's blood ran cold. Surely the magistrate wouldn't believe Slushman. Surely Isaac could prove that Slushman's accusations were false, that he was lying.

Spencer leaned over and whispered in Emma's ear, "Don't worry."

"What if the magistrate believes him, Spencer? Everyone else seems to."

"That's because they don't know you. Isaac hasn't had a chance to tell them what you are like."

Emma tried to be brave, to put on a confident front, but no matter how hard she tried, she couldn't stop the tears from streaming down her cheeks.

"Do you have anything else to add, Lord Slushman?" the magistrate asked.

"No, your honor. I have every confidence that you will do what is right and remove this killer from polite society so she cannot attempt to kill more people."

The magistrate nodded his agreement. "It's gratifying to see that you have recovered from your grievous injuries, Lord Slushman."

The magistrate's conciliatory tone sent shivers down Emma's spine. The man was sympathetic toward that rogue! That did not bode well for her.

The wigged judge turned to where she sat with Isaac and Spencer. "Is your counsel here?" he asked.

"Yes," Isaac said. "My name is Isaac Reynolds, Earl of Wistrom, solicitor at large. I will be representing Miss Sullivan."

"Very well. Do you agree with the details of the night in question as described by Viscount Slushman?"

"Not at all, your honor. Lord Slushman's accounting of the events of that night are all fabrications and vicious lies."

"Your honor," Slushman said, rising to his feet. "Don't tell me the court will take the word of a commoner over that of a peer of the realm?"

"No, Lord Slushman. The court intends to take the word of the party that is telling the truth."

"That is reassuring, then, because I am the one telling the truth."

"That remains to be seen, Lord Slushman," the magistrate said, then turned back to Isaac. "Continue, Lord Wistrom."

"Thank you, your honor. As I was saying, Miss Sullivan disagrees with nearly everything Lord Slushman related."

"Such as?"

"First of all, Slushman wasn't in conversation with an upstairs maid on the evening in question. He had accosted her with nefarious intent."

"And what was this nefarious intent?"

"Rape, your honor."

The courtroom erupted in loud jeers and cries of denial.

"That's a lie!" Slushman argued. "I would never rape a member of my mother's staff. Or rather, that is to say, I would never rape *any* person. Ever. It's absolutely preposterous!"

"But indeed you have, Lord Slushman," Isaac shouted, interrupting the man's tirade. "May I suggest that you have upon numerous occasions done that exact crime to numerous staff members employed by your mother?"

"Lies!" Slushman cried out in horror. "I would never."

"And yet you have!" Isaac bellowed.

"Then where is this woman? Bring her forward so that I can face her."

"I shouldn't have to. Just know that I have her sworn statement attesting to your attack and your intent."

"Then she is lying!" Slushman said with more force.

"No, my husband is not lying," Janey said, rising to her feet.

Slushman turned to face her. "Husband? Who is your husband?"

"Isaac Reynolds, Earl of Wistrom. I am Lady Wistrom, Countess Wistrom. And you, Lord Slushman, attacked and attempted to rape me."

The courtroom erupted into a buzz of anger that was no doubt heard throughout half of London.

"Liar!" Slushman hollered. "I have never raped anyone in my life. I don't have to. Women throw themselves at my feet!"

"If you have never raped anyone in your mother's employ, why are there so many women who were let go when they were found to be with child?" Isaac asked.

"If they were with child, the child was not mine!"

"Then why did these women go to Scotland Yard to bring charges of rape against you? They named you, sir. They named *you*! Why do you think that is?"

"How should I know? No doubt they were simply disgruntled employees who were let go because they did not meet my mother's high standards."

"And why, Lord Slushman, were these women found living on the streets, all with bastards with your same features—curly red hair and striking blue eyes?"

"I dare you to find one child who matches that description," Slushman blustered.

Isaac turned to the door of the courtroom and nodded to the Marquess of Revelow. He opened the door, and the Earl of Marsten led one lass after another into the courtroom. Each lass held in her arms a babe, or led by the hand a child. Each child had bright red hair and startling blue eyes, just like Lord Slushman—their father.

"Who do you have here?" the magistrate asked when the last lass had entered the courtroom.

Isaac stepped to the first female in the line before the magistrate. "Each of these women worked for Lady Pearlman as upstairs maids and were let go because they were found to be with child. As you can see, their children all had the same father."

"You can't prove that," Slushman said. "You could have advertised for any female with a child with red hair and blue eyes."

"I could have, yes, but I didn't. Over the past five years, each of these women has filed a complaint with Scotland Yard stating that she had been raped by Viscount Slushman." Isaac stepped forward and laid the letters of complaint on the magistrate's desk.

The spectators in the courtroom erupted in a cacophony of foot stomping and boos and jeers and yelling, and calling Slushman every vile and derogatory name they could.

The magistrate pounded his gavel again and again to get order in his court, but it took several warnings to the crowd. When order was finally restored, the magistrate spoke to the girls.

"Ladies, please tell the court your name and that of your child, and confirm that what Lord Wistrom accused Lord Slushman of doing actually occurred."

The first young lady did exactly as she was instructed and stated her name and that of her son. She gave his age as four years and affirmed that Slushman had indeed raped her. She confirmed that she'd been dismissed from Lady Pearlman's employ without a letter of recommendation and without any money to support her child.

The crowd again burst into raucous boos and jeers.

The magistrate pounded his gavel, but the crowd was getting angrier by the minute. The magistrate picked up the complaint papers, came down from the bench, and walked along the row of women, asking their names, the names of their children, and confirming that they had been raped by Slushman.

The last in the line was a lass by the name of Dolly Patterson, and she had no child with her.

"Where's your child, Dolly?"

"She's no longer with us, your honor. She went to live with the angels. She died when she was but four months old."

"How did she die?" he asked.

"She got sick, and I couldn't afford to buy any medicine to make her well. I went to Lady Pearlman, but she said she didn't remember me working for her and sent me away."

There were sobs and tears from almost everyone in the gallery at the sad tales from the lasses that Slushman had abused then tossed to the side.

When the magistrate had heard from all the women, he went back to his chair. "Miss Sullivan?"

Isaac motioned for Emma to stand and face the magistrate. She did.

"Miss Sullivan, do you admit to stabbing Lord Slushman with a letter opener?"

Emma looked at Isaac, and he nodded. "Yes."

"Would you explain in your own words why you did something so heinous?"

"I attacked Lord Slushman because he was practically strangling my friend in his attempt to rape her, and I had to stop him."

"I see. That was a very dangerous thing to do, don't you think?"

"Perhaps, but not as horrific as what would have happened to Janey if I hadn't done anything."

The magistrate sat back in his chair and folded his arms over his chest. The expression on his face was cold as ice. Isaac had told her this magistrate had a reputation for handing down the harshest sentences for any wrongdoing. She studied the glare in his eyes and didn't doubt that was true.

Emma stood while the magistrate considered the severity of the sentence he intended to hand down. The longer he took, the weaker every limb in her body became. Her legs buckled beneath her, and she lost her balance.

Spencer stood and wrapped his arm around her to keep her from collapsing. Emma had never needed anything as desperately as she needed his strength to help her at this moment.

"Miss Sullivan," the magistrate said, leaning forward in his chair and focusing his intense glare on her. "I find you innocent of any and all charges leveled against you by your accuser. You have the court's apology for what you have endured."

The onlookers in the gallery broke out in thunderous cheers and applause. The magistrate's verdict was so unexpected that Emma collapsed in Spencer's arms.

The magistrate didn't even try to quiet the crowd in the courtroom. He let them applaud until their boisterous cheers died down.

"Are you all right, Emma?" Spencer asked, holding her close and kissing her on the forehead.

"Is it over?" she asked.

"Yes, it's over, and you are free." A fresh river of tears ran down her face, and Spencer removed a clean handkerchief from his pocket to dry them. "I love you, Emma," he said, giving her another kiss on the cheek.

She looked over Spencer's shoulder and saw Isaac and Janey beside him. "Thank you, Isaac. Thank you, Janey. This is over, and I am free because of you. How can I ever repay you?"

"You already have," Isaac said. "You repaid me when you brought Janey back to me."

All of a sudden, the magistrate pounded his gavel to get everyone's attention. "This court is not adjourned," he shouted to be heard over the noise.

Gradually, the people in the gallery quieted and took their seats.

"Lord Slushman," the magistrate announced. "You will rise and face the court."

Slushman rose to his feet and faced the bench with the most pompous expression Emma had ever seen. It turned her stomach to the point that she could not even look at him, or she feared she might be ill.

"You are responsible for the greatest share in this travesty and will be held responsible for what you have done. Do you have anything to say for yourself?"

"I cannot imagine that I had anything to do with what happened," Slushman replied. "*I* am the victim in this travesty, as you called it. *I* am the one who was stabbed and nearly died. *I* am the one whose name is maligned and sullied, and *I* am the one who will forever have to try to repair my good name to be able to walk about in Society with my head held high. No, I cannot imagine anything for which I need to answer."

His honor sat with his mouth ajar for a few moments. "Then it is obvious you have learned nothing from what has happened today, and I feel sorry for you, because you will no doubt not understand the punishment you are about to receive."

"Punishment?"

"Yes. I see six beautiful children who are here because of your misdeeds and abandoned because of your neglect. There is no doubt of their parentage or your responsibility for them. I order you to pay each mother one hundred pounds to support and care for them. And two hundred pounds to the mother who lost her child because she could not afford to feed or care for her babe."

"That's not fair!" Slushman called out as the crowd cheered their approval.

"And I sentence you to one month hard labor in the workhouse to work off the debt your father will no doubt have to cover for you."

"No!" Slushman bellowed.

Emma was sure he had never worked even one hour in his life, let alone executed a month of hard labor. She didn't know how he would ever survive such punishment.

"I am the person who was attacked and nearly died. I should not be the one punished!"

"Enough," the magistrate ordered Slushman as he pounded his gavel. "Or I will make it two months of hard labor. Now," he said to the officers of the court. "Take him away."

Agents of Scotland Yard approached Slushman and led him from the court as he bellowed in protest. Before he left, he paused in front of Emma and glared at her.

"You will pay for this," he said as the officers pushed him forward.

"Don't pay him any mind," Spencer said, pulling her close and shielding her from more vile comments from Slushman.

The magistrate announced that court was dismissed, then the people filed out.

"Here," Spencer said, leading her to a chair. "Sit down for a bit before you fall down."

Emma sat. "I am a little weak," she said.

"When was the last time you ate anything?" Janey asked.

Emma shook her head. "I can't remember. It's been days."

"We need to get something in your stomach, then," Spencer said. "Let's go to my townhouse. Cook will have something prepared for us. It may not be a huge meal, but we can at least have cold meats and cheeses and bread."

"That sounds wonderful," Emma said as she stood.

"Lord Carnhaven," Inspector Whitaker said from beside them. "Congratulations, and thank you. On behalf of the lasses who were abused and abandoned, I thank you."

"You are welcome," Spencer replied.

"I honestly didn't think you'd be able to pull this one off, but you did. You were brilliant. And you, Miss Sullivan, are one very lucky lady."

"I know I am, Inspector," Emma said with a smile. She looked up at Spencer, and her smile grew brighter. "I am one *very* lucky lady."

CHAPTER FOURTEEN

WHEN THEY LEFT the court, they went to Spencer's townhouse. Everyone involved in proving Emma innocent, including the Earl of Marsten, Marquess of Revelow, and two other friends of Spencer's, joined them. Even Inspector Whitaker came. The women and children who had testified were also invited, but had already arranged their own celebration at a nearby establishment.

"The female population of London owes you a great debt, Carnhaven," Whitaker said.

"Do you think Slushman will change his ways?" Emma asked.

"Do you want my honest opinion?" Whitaker said. "No, I don't think there's a chance. He can't even admit he did anything wrong."

Emma reached for Spencer's hand and held it. "How sad."

"Don't worry, Emma," he said. "You're safe now."

And she knew she was—at least for a month.

She listened to the conversations going on around her but couldn't bring herself to become involved in any of them. How could she, when that month would go by so quickly?

It was quite late in the evening before their guests left and Isaac and Janey went up to the room prepared for them. Emma was finally alone with Spencer.

"Are you terribly tired?" he asked. He wrapped his arm

around her shoulders and pulled her close to him.

"I should be, but I'm not. Today was too tumultuous a day."

"Would you like to get some air?"

"I'd love to," she answered.

Spencer led her out the double French doors and onto a small terrace. He escorted her to a bench on the far edge where they sat surrounded by blooming shrubbery.

"Oh, it's a beautiful night," she said, wrapping her arm around Spencer's waist and nestling as close to him as she could.

Spencer placed his arm around her shoulder. She looked up at him, and he lowered his head and kissed her.

His kiss was filled with passion and hinted at all the emotions he felt for her. "I love you, Emma. More than I thought I could ever love anyone again. I was convinced of it when I feared I might lose you. I knew then that I couldn't survive without you."

Emma clasped her palms to his cheeks, brought his face down to hers, and pressed her lips to his. His kiss was deep and intense before he lifted his mouth from hers, slid to a knee in front of her, and held her hands.

"I love you Emma, and don't want to live one more day without you. My love, will you marry me?"

Tears filled Emma's eyes and her heart swelled in her breast. She loved Spencer more than life itself. "Of course I will, Spencer. It would be the greatest honor of my life to become your wife."

A smile lit his face, and he slid onto the bench beside her, then pressed his lips to hers and kissed her hungrily. When he broke their kiss, he reached into his pocket, took out a small blue velvet box, and opened it.

"This was my mother's. I'd like you to wear it, if you like it."

Emma looked at the beautiful opal surrounded by tiny diamonds, and the gorgeous ring swam before her eyes. "Oh, Spencer. It's beautiful. I love it."

"I'm glad you like it."

"How could I not?"

Spencer took her in his arms and held her close. "When do

you want to marry?"

Emma lifted her gaze and gave him a teasing smile. "Tomorrow?"

He laughed. "Very well. That can be arranged."

Emma couldn't hide her shocked expression. "I wasn't serious, Spencer."

"But I was." He reached into his jacket pocket and handed her a piece of paper.

Emma took it and looked at it in the moonlight. "Is this a special license?"

"I obtained it when you were in prison. I knew then that whether or not you were freed, I was going to marry you. I was never going to let you out of my sight again."

"Oh, I love you," Emma said, then kissed him with all the passion she had to offer him.

"The only question is, do we want to marry here, or in Willowbrook?" he asked.

"I want to get married in Willowbrook. I want your girls to be with us when we marry. They need to be a part of the event."

"Of course they do," Spencer agreed. "Cassie and Felicity would never forgive us if we married without them."

"Now, the only question I have," Emma said, "is how soon can we go home?"

Spencer lowered his head and kissed her. "Is tomorrow soon enough?"

"That's perfect," Emma answered, and wrapped her arms around his neck. "Love me, Spencer," she whispered.

"I do," he replied. "You know I do."

"No. Make love to me."

"Are you sure you don't want to wait?"

"I've never been more sure of anything in my life," she answered, and let him lead her back indoors and to his bedroom.

He closed the door and locked it, then slowly undressed her. Once he had shed his own clothing, he laid her on the bed and lay next to her.

Their lovemaking wasn't perfect the first time—awkward and hesitant in small ways. But neither of them found fault, only encouragement to explore further. They began a lifetime of joy discovering the ways of loving that would please them most.

SPENCER AND EMMA didn't leave the next morning like he wanted to. Emma had a list of gifts she wanted to take home with her. She didn't know when she'd get back to London again, and there were several items she couldn't get in Willowbrook.

One place she wanted to go was the bookstore. She wanted to see if there were books the girls might enjoy that they might not find at the Page Turner in Willowbrook.

She also wanted to take Cassie a fresh supply of watercolors and paper. And Felicity was in need of a riding habit. Spencer mentioned it was time she had a horse of her own and learned to ride. Emma knew that would thrill her to no end.

And she wanted to get each girl a necklace to commemorate her marriage to their father. Something special that they could wear to the wedding and beyond.

They spent the day shopping for anything they couldn't get in Willowbrook, then rose early the next morning and started their journey home. Isaac and Janey followed them.

"I can't believe how anxious I am to get home," Emma said. "It seems as if we've been gone months instead of just days."

"I know what you mean," Spencer said, reaching out to hold her hand. "And they were days I'd prefer not to relive ever again."

"With one recent exception, of course." Emma smiled coquettishly. She coughed demurely and resumed a more sober expression. "Do you wonder how Slushman is faring?"

"I try not to," Spencer answered. "But I can't help but think about him. I'm sure he's not having an easy time adjusting to such a radical change."

"The inspector doesn't think he'll be reformed when all is said and done."

Spencer placed the backs of his fingers on her cheek and let them travel down to her jaw. "I don't either, Em."

She snuggled closer to him. "What do you think he'll do when his month is over?"

"Don't worry about him, my dearest. You are safe now. I'll take care of you."

"I know, Spencer. I'm not worried."

But she was. She couldn't help but remember what Slushman said as he left the courtroom.

"You'll pay for this."

CHAPTER FIFTEEN

THE LAST MONTH had been the happiest, most brilliant month of Emma's life. She married Spencer in a small, private wedding, with Janey standing up with her, and Isaac standing up with Spencer. Cassandra and Felicity also stood with them. They walked down the aisle ahead of Emma and scattered flower petals for her to walk on.

Everything about the day was absolutely perfect, and when they went to bed that night, she was Emma Washburn, Countess of Carnhaven.

Two weeks after their wedding, Isaac and Janey came with the news that they were expecting their first child. Janey was certain it was a boy, but Isaac hoped it was a girl. He wanted a little girl who looked exactly like Janey, but then admitted he would be overjoyed with either a boy or a girl, as long as it was happy and healthy.

The best news of the summer was the expression on Felicity's face when the local seamstress finished her riding habit and Spencer presented her with her very own pony. She named it Joy because she was "over-Joyed" to get it.

"Shall we ride today?" Spencer asked them at breakfast one morning. There was a broad smile on his face because he knew no one would turn down his offer.

"Oh, yes, Papa," Felicity cried out, placing her napkin beside her plate and rising to her feet.

Emma couldn't hold back her laughter. There was nothing she enjoyed more than going for a ride with her family. When she was a governess, she remembered thinking that she would probably never have children of her own, but here she was with two daughters. Even if they were not children from her body, they were her children, and in time there would be more. Unless she was mistaken, it would be sooner rather than later. She had already missed this month's menses by almost a week, and unless it came in the next few days, that meant she was carrying a babe. At this rate, Spencer could give her a dozen or more in short order.

"Run upstairs, girls, and put on your riding habits."

They both leaped away at an unladylike pace, but Emma let their lack of decorum go unchecked. She didn't want to dampen their enthusiasm.

"Aren't you going with us, Em?" Spencer asked.

"I think I'll remain here. I have some letters I want to write, and I don't feel quite right."

"Is something wrong?"

"No, no. I'm just a little tired, that's all. And you have only yourself to blame for that."

Spencer gave a hearty laugh. "I suppose I do," he said, rising to his feet and kissing her cheek. "But you will be excused this once. It will be well worth letting you stay home and rest while the rest of us leave you in peace."

"How generous of you," Emma said, relishing another kiss.

"We'll be back in an hour or so," he said when he heard the girls scramble down the stairs. And he left the house with his daughters.

Emma watched them walk to the stable together, then ride off through the meadow. Spencer was an excellent rider and was teaching both of his daughters well. She could imagine the day when they would go to London and he would proudly escort them through Hyde Park.

Emma went to one of the drawing rooms and reclined on a sofa. She didn't want to go upstairs because she didn't want to miss her family's return. She pulled a shawl over herself and fell asleep immediately.

AT THE FRINGES of her drowsy state, Emma heard something that caused her to stir. It sounded like a scuffle coming from the foyer.

She rose from the sofa and opened the door. From there she couldn't see clearly what had happened, but it looked as though their butler was lying on the floor.

"Jasper!" she yelped, and ran across the foyer. She knelt down when she reached him, but a familiar voice stopped her and strong fingers clamped around her arms.

"Don't worry about your butler, slut. You have bigger problems to concern yourself with."

Emma's blood turned to ice and a terror unlike anything she'd experienced before caused her breath to catch.

"You didn't think I'd forgotten about you, did you?"

Emma couldn't answer him. She couldn't find her voice.

"You were all I could think of while I was in that workhouse." Slushman backed her up and threw her against the wall. Emma's head hit with such force that her world threatened to slither away. "Fourteen hours a day, all I could think about was how I was going to pay you back for what you did to me."

"I didn't do anything to you, Slushman. You got what you deserved for what you did to all those women. For what you would have continued to do if you hadn't been stopped." Before she could prepare herself for what he intended to do, he pulled back his arm and slammed his fist into her face.

"You don't know half of what you did, bitch! You destroyed my life." He pulled his arm back and hit her again. "You not only ruined my life, but you ruined my entire family's lives."

"I didn't ruin their lives," Emma countered. "*You* that did when you took advantage of all those innocent women who worked for your mother."

"Those were servants! They are barely human. They are ignorant, uneducated peasants. They are nothing!"

"How dare you consider them as nothing," Emma said, pulling away from him. "They are each worth more than a dozen of your kind."

"Well, because of you, *my kind* has turned their backs on me and my family. My mother hasn't received an invitation to one event since my trial. My father and I are no longer welcome in any of our clubs, and my sisters have no hope of making a match this Season or next. My mother and father are even talking about leaving London and going to America. All because of you!"

"You can't see the part you played in this travesty, can you?" Emma said, wiping at the blood that dripped from her chin.

"I played no part in this devastation. It's entirely your fault. You made everything seem so much worse than it was. And now you'll pay for what you did."

Emma struggled to get out of Slushman's grasp, but he tightened his hold on her. She thought she might have a chance to escape, but he pulled a gun from his pocket and held it against her ribs.

A split second later, he lifted the gun in the air and fired it.

"That should get him here faster," Slushman said with a malevolent laugh. At Emma's surprised expression, he laughed again. "You didn't think I'd let him live, did you? Not after what he did to me!"

"No!"

SPENCER COULDN'T GET over how much his daughters had improved over the past month and a half. Of course, they'd gone riding every day, either with him or with Emma. She was turning into an accomplished rider, and the girls were equally as talented.

"Do you want to race to the hedgerow, Papa?" Felicity asked.

"I would love to," he answered, "but we are not going to jump the hedge today. I lost five years of my life the last time you jumped the hedge without telling me you were going to do that."

Felicity looked at Cassie, and they both laughed.

"I didn't think that was a bit funny, girls. You could have fallen and broken your necks."

"We're too good to do something so reckless," Felicity said.

"Tell me that when you end up with a broken arm or leg," Spencer replied.

"Very well, Papa," Cassie said. "We'll be careful."

They got ready to race, but Felicity stopped them. "Who is that, Papa?" she said, pointing to their right.

"I don't know," Spencer answered. "You girls stay here and I'll see what they want. Whoever it is seems to be in a big hurry."

He raced away to meet the group of riders. As he got closer, he recognized Inspector Whitaker and three Scotland Yard agents.

His heart thundered in his chest, and he wished Emma would have ridden with them. He needed her to be with him so he could make sure she was safe.

"Inspector," Spencer called, but before he got the greeting out, he knew something was wrong. "He's out, isn't he?"

"Yes. And he's making threats. Is your wife with you?"

"No, she's in the house. The girls are with me."

"We need to get to her, now," Whitaker said, but Spencer was already racing toward the house.

"Girls, stay here," Spencer bellowed over his shoulder.

"Foster," Inspector Whitaker yelled. "Stay with the girls."

Just then, Spencer heard it. A single gunshot coming from the house. He spurred his horse to race as fast as he could go. Whitaker and two agents followed closely behind.

Spencer had never been so frightened—except for that fateful day five years earlier when he lost the mother of his daughters. He felt as though he was reliving that same nightmare all over again.

Emma was an unexpected gift he never thought he'd receive. He never thought he would be blessed with a love as precious and rare as his first. But he had. He woke up every morning feeling as if he was waking from the most spectacular dream. He wasn't sure if he could survive losing a love so rare a second time.

Spencer pushed his horse to go even faster. His heart pounded as wildly as his horse's hooves thundered over the hard ground. They hadn't ridden that far from Carnhaven Manor, yet it seemed as if they were miles away.

Spencer pulled his horse up hard as they entered the courtyard. He vaulted from the horse's back and then forced himself to slow down. It was simple caution that kept him from running frantically into the house. He dared not be the reason Slushman panicked and killed Emma.

"Do you see him?" Whitaker asked.

"No, but something is wrong. Do you see any stable hands? They should be busy tending to their work, but there's not one around."

Whitaker slowed next to him, his pistol drawn.

"Cover me," Spencer said, and took his first step toward the manor house.

"Well, imagine seeing you here," Slushman's voice rang out from inside the house. "We didn't think you would ever return, did we, Miss Sullivan?"

Slushman emerged from the front door, pushing Emma out in front of him, and Spencer got his first look at his wife's bloody and bruised face. He was consumed with rage. "You are a dead man," he roared.

"I've already died a thousand deaths, Carnhaven. Going to bed every night, I prayed I wouldn't wake in the morning, yet somehow I did."

"Let her go," Spencer demanded. "Let her go and I'll let you live."

"As what?" Slushman asked. "She made me a pariah. I'm banned from all my clubs. Even my friends won't talk to me. My parents have been ostracized. They're not welcome at any social events, and my sisters don't stand a chance of having their come-out or making a decent match. You and she have done this to me."

"We didn't do this to you, Slushman. You did this to yourself. Look at the number of lives you ruined."

"Those lives hardly matter! What is my life or that of my sisters, compared to the life of a lowly upstairs maid? What is my reputation, compared to that of someone from the gutter?"

"Those innocent girls are worth a lot more than you will ever be," Spencer growled at him.

It was obvious that Slushman was losing his temper. Obvious that he had no intention of being reasoned with. Obvious that he didn't care if he came out alive from this confrontation. What Spencer didn't know was who else wouldn't come out alive.

"Let her go, Slushman. Send her over to me unharmed and I'll let you walk away from here."

"You have no idea how enticing that sounds. Except for one thing. All I dreamed of twenty-four hours a day the entire time I spent in that hellhole was making her pay for what she did to me."

"No, she didn't do that to you!" Spencer argued. "You did that to yourself."

"No!" Slushman said, then raised his pistol and pointed it at Emma's head.

"No!" Spencer yelled. "Don't do it!"

For a second, he thought Slushman actually intended to let Emma go. That he intended to let Emma live. The reprobate released his wife and pushed her toward Spencer.

She didn't have the strength to stay on her feet and run, but she at least was strong enough to hold herself up as she staggered toward him.

"Spencer," she cried out in a weak voice. "I love you."

"Emma," he called out as he reached for her. He almost had her in his arms when the first shot exploded, and Spencer saw the expression on her face turn to disbelief, then shock. "Emma!" he cried out as he reached for her.

Her body went limp in his arms as an explosion of gunfire erupted all around him. Whitaker and his agents fired at Slushman, who didn't stand a chance. He was dead before he hit the ground.

"Someone go for a doctor," Spencer yelled as he lifted Emma in his arms and carried her to the house. She was bleeding badly, but he refused to admit that the amount of blood she was losing could kill her.

She couldn't die. He wouldn't let her.

He carried her up the stairs to the room where they'd made such passionate love the night before, and placed her on the bed.

"Stay with me, Em. Don't you dare die. I couldn't survive if you left me, and neither could the girls."

Maids rushed in and out of the room with basins of water and armloads of towels and salves and bandages, and anything else the doctor might need. Spencer sat beside Emma and pressed a cloth to her shoulder to slow the flow of blood, but he wasn't sure it was helping.

He continued to talk to her without stopping. Hopefully, she could hear him and stay anchored by his voice. That was the only thing he could think of to do. He was losing her. He knew he was. She hadn't as much as moaned in pain since she was shot.

"Emma?" he whispered. "Emma?" He leaned over her and kissed her cheek. Her face had already started to turn black and blue, even as her lady's maid washed the blood from her face. Tears fell from the young woman's eyes while she cared for Emma.

"The doctor will be here any minute, Emma. He'll take care of you and you'll be fine in no time." Spencer took a fresh cloth and pressed it against the wound. "I think the bullet went through your shoulder, Emma. That's good. At least Dr. Edwards won't have to dig it out."

He cleaned as much blood from around the wound as he could. Before he'd done much, the door opened and Dr. Edwards hurried into the room. A second doctor followed him.

"Dr. Edwards! Thank God you're here! My wife has been shot!"

"Lord Carnhaven, this is my partner, Dr. Rutherford." Dr. Edwards stepped closer to Emma, and Spencer gave him room to work.

"Has she spoken since she was shot?"

"No. She hasn't said anything."

"That's not uncommon. Your wife is in shock. Now," he said. "Why don't you leave us for a while? I'll be down to speak with you when we know more."

"I'd prefer to stay here," Spencer said, reaching for Emma's hand.

"I know you would, my lord, but we just need to see what we're dealing with. You can come back when we know something."

"Very well," Spencer said. He kissed Emma again and told her he loved her before he left, then walked out of the room on legs that threatened not to hold him up.

He took the stairs one by one, but only managed to go a third of the way down before he collapsed on a step and buried his head in his hands. He tried to remain strong, but he lost his battle and cried as hard as he had when he lost Caroline.

CHAPTER SIXTEEN

SPENCER SOBBED UNTIL he had no more tears to cry, then went down the remainder of the stairs. Cassandra and Felicity were huddled together on a sofa in the library with their arms wrapped around each other.

"How is Mama?" they both asked as they raced into his arms.

"The doctor said he'd come down and talk to us when he knows more," he told them as he hugged them back. "Come here," he said, leading them to the sofa and sitting with Cassandra on one side of him and Felicity on the other.

"Has she said anything?" Cassandra asked. "I heard one of the servants tell another one that she hasn't said anything since that man came in the house. Why did he want to hurt her?"

"Because he was sick, Cassie. He was a very cruel man, and he blamed Mama for everything bad that happened to him."

"But she didn't do anything bad to him, did she?"

"No, Felicity. Mama only protected Lady Jane when he tried to do something bad to her."

"But why did he blame Mama if she was only protecting Lady Jane?"

"Because when something bad happens and we aren't strong enough to blame ourselves, we think we'll feel better if we blame someone else."

"Why would he do that?"

"Because that man was sick, and he didn't want to admit that what happened was his own fault."

"Oh," Cassandra said. Felicity just sat beside him with a serious expression on her face.

Consoling words rose to the tip of his tongue, and as he spoke them, the door opened and Dr. Edwards entered the room. Spencer rose and faced the doctor. Cassandra and Felicity stood at his sides. They each slipped one of their small hands into his and squeezed his fingers.

"How is she, doctor?"

"She will be fine."

Spencer fought back the tears that filled his eyes and wanted to spill down his cheeks. "Thank you, Dr. Edwards. Thank you."

His daughters wrapped their arms around his waist and sobbed.

"You can go up to see her in a few minutes. She's awake now, but will probably sleep off and on for a few days."

Spencer nodded, then turned to his daughters. "Girls, let me go up to see Emma first. Go to the kitchen and get something to eat. I know you haven't eaten anything since breakfast. You can go up after I've had a chance to talk to your mother."

"Yes, Papa," they answered, and left the room.

Spencer turned to the doctor. "There's more, isn't there, Dr. Edwards?"

"Yes."

"Have a seat, please," he said, then walked across the room and filled two glasses with brandy. He gave the doctor a glass, then sat down.

"Yes?" Spencer asked. "It's the reason she wouldn't wake, isn't it?"

"Yes," the doctor answered. "Your wife may have willed herself into deep shock out of fear the man who attacked her was going to rape her. As I understand it, she knew that he had done that to numerous women before."

"Yes," Spencer answered. "And did he?"

"No. There are no signs of your wife having been raped. There is proof that the intruder beat her. She has numerous bruises on her face and arms, but no sign that she was raped."

"Thank God," Spencer said.

"Now, unless you have any questions, you may go up to see your wife."

"Thank you, Dr. Edwards. I'll have someone show you to the kitchen, and you can join my daughters for something to eat. And I'll send Dr. Rutherford down to join you."

Dr. Edwards thanked him, but Spencer was already out of the room and halfway up the stairs and didn't hear everything he said. He took the stairs two at a time and stopped to catch his breath when he reached Emma's room. He reached for the handle to her door and opened it.

He had an idea what to expect, but he wasn't prepared for the bruises that covered her face. They were much darker than before, and covered a much greater area.

Spencer rushed to where Emma lay and kissed her forehead. "Don't you ever frighten me like that again, Em. My heart won't take it."

"I won't," she whispered. "I promise." She tried to smile, but he could tell how difficult it was for her.

Just then, a footman entered the room and took Dr. Rutherford down to join Dr. Edwards. When Spencer and Emma were alone, he turned back to her and took her hand.

"Dr. Edwards said you are going to be fine. That you will need plenty of rest for the next few weeks, but you will make a full recovery."

"What else did he tell you?"

"You always do get right to the point, don't you, Em?"

"Yes, it's better to face everything than put it off. What else did he tell you?"

"He said that Slushman did not rape you. And that you went into shock because you were afraid that he was going to and you didn't want to remember any of it. Is that about it?"

"One more thing," she said. "Do you believe him?"

"Of course I believe him. Why wouldn't I?"

"No reason at all. I just wanted to hear you say it."

"And do you believe me?"

"Yes," Emma answered with a great sigh.

"Have I told you lately that I love you?" Spencer asked. He sat on the edge of the bed and held her hand.

"Yes, you have, but that seems a lifetime ago."

Spencer couldn't help but smile. "It does, doesn't it? So I'd better tell you again so you don't forget. I love you, Em. With all my heart."

"And I love you, Spencer. I was so afraid Slushman was going to kill me, and I'd never see you again, or that I'd never have the opportunity to tell you how much I loved you."

"Then we'd better tell each other often how much we love each other."

"Yes. We'd better. I love you, Spencer."

"I love you, Em. And I always will."

CHAPTER SEVENTEEN

EMMA OPENED HER eyes and focused on Spencer. He sat in the chair and slept. Her heart swelled in her breast. He was the dearest man she'd ever known, and he was her husband.

As if he realized she was watching him, he opened his eyes and focused on her. A smile lit his face.

"How do you feel?"

"Better. I think I can get up for a little while today, and perhaps watch the girls ride."

"And I don't think you will. It's only been a little over a week since you were shot."

"But I really need to get up and get some exercise," she protested. "I'm going to get bed sores if I remain in bed another day. This is making me very lazy."

"That's how I want you."

"You want me lazy?"

"Yes, if that will make you heal faster," he said.

"I would like you to do me one favor, though, Spencer."

"Of course, Em. What do you want?"

"I would like you to send someone for Dr. Edwards. There's no hurry. I'd just like to ask him a question." Emma saw a look of concern cover his features. "Nothing is wrong, Spence. I just have a question I need to ask him, and I know you won't take me into town."

"No carriage rides for you yet, my dear. I'll send someone into town right away."

Spencer walked to the door to do what she'd asked, then stopped. "Are you sure there's nothing wrong, Em?"

"I'm positive, Spencer," she said with a smile. "Now, don't worry."

SPENCER PACED THE floor without stopping except to take another swallow from his glass of brandy. He couldn't figure out what was taking Dr. Edwards so long with Emma. Something must be wrong.

"Papa?" Cassandra said as she and Felicity rushed into the room. "Why is Dr. Edwards here? Is something wrong with Mama?"

Spencer placed his arms around their shoulders and held them close. "I don't know. She only asked me to send for Dr. Edwards. She said there was nothing wrong, but I can't imagine why she'd need to see a doctor if nothing was wrong."

"Maybe she just wants the doctor to tell you she is well enough to get out of bed and sit outside," Felicity said.

"Do you think so?" Cassie asked, clearly doubting her sister's reasoning.

"Listen," Spencer said. "I think I hear the doctor coming."

They turned to face the door.

"You were correct, Lady Carnhaven," Dr. Edwards said as he emerged. "Your family looks as though I'm going to deliver news of your impending death."

"I told you," Em said with a wink, then walked to her family and gave them each a boisterous kiss. "I have some news I want to share with you, but I felt I should check with Dr. Edwards before saying anything—just to make sure I'm not mistaken."

"What news?" Cassandra asked.

"Lady Carnhaven is going to have a baby," Dr. Edwards announced.

The room was silent for a few moments, then filled with shrieks of joy. The girls couldn't be happier. Spencer was in shock.

"Girls," Emma said. "Please, run down to the kitchen and have Cook prepare a tea tray."

"Yes, Mama," they said, and ran from the room.

"Already?" Spencer asked when the girls were gone.

"That's what I thought, too, which was why I needed a second opinion."

"And I have confirmed your wife's suspicions," Dr. Edwards said.

"I can't believe this," Spencer said, reaching for his wife and kissing her.

"Well, believe it," Emma said. "In about seven months, you will hopefully welcome your Carnhaven heir."

"Girl or boy," Spencer said, "it doesn't matter to me what it is, as long as it's healthy and well."

Emma wrapped her arms around Spencer's waist and held him. Just then, the girls came in pushing a tea tray with more cakes and pastries than a small army could eat.

"I take it you told the kitchen staff our happy news?" Emma said.

"You should have heard them," Cassie said. "They were as excited as we are."

"I believe it. I can still hear them," Emma said. "Cassie, would you pour?"

"Yes, Mama. I'm happy to."

Emma lifted her gaze, and her eyes locked with her husband's. His were filled with tears.

Their family was growing by leaps and bounds. And their daughters were growing faster than she and Spencer could keep up with.

Emma had never been happier.

EPILOGUE

"WOULD YOU LIKE to go for a walk in the garden, Em?" Spencer asked his wife. She seemed a little nervous today. Not her usual relaxed self.

"I think I would love to go for a walk. That sounds like the perfect thing to do."

Spencer extended his arm, and Emma took his hand and let him pull her to her feet. They walked out the French doors onto the terrace, then down the three steps and down the center path in the garden. When they reached the pond, they sat on a bench opposite the water and watched the ducks swim past.

"Isn't this relaxing?" Emma said, shifting on the bench.

"Are you uncomfortable?"

"Not uncomfortable, really. Just… Oh, I don't know. I seem to have a backache."

"A backache?" Spencer asked.

"Yes. Is that significant? You are the one who went through this before with the girls' mother."

"Well, it may be."

"What does it mean?"

"Perhaps nothing. And perhaps it means we should return to the house," he said, holding out his hand to take hers.

Spencer took her hand and helped her to her feet. She'd barely taken one step when her water broke.

"Oh!"

"Yes, that is often what it means. We'd best get you to your room and send for the doctor."

"Is the baby coming, Spencer?"

"Yes, I think it is."

"Oh," Emma said, then walked with Spencer up the stairs. They'd barely reached the third step when she was struck with a searing pain that doubled her over. "Ohh!" she cried out.

Spencer reached down and scooped her into his arms.

"Ohh!" she cried again.

Spencer carried her to the top of the stairs as gently and as quickly as he could. He had to stop several more times when a birthing pain seized her. He finally reached the top of the stairs and carried her to their suite of rooms.

"Have someone watch for the doctor, Helen," he ordered the maid. "And send him up right away."

"Yes, my lord."

"And anything he will need."

"Yes, my lord."

"You won't leave me alone, will you, Spence?" Emma said between gasps.

"No, sweetheart. Not if you don't want me to."

"No, I don't want you—oh!—to leave me."

Spencer reached for her hand and held it as one pain after another grabbed her.

"I think our baby's coming, Spencer," she cried out.

His heart raced in his chest. "I think it would be better if you wait until the doctor arrives, Emma."

"I'm not sure I…can!" she cried as she squeezed his hand with all her might.

Spencer jumped from the bed and opened the door. "Helen!"

"Yes, my lord?" the maid answered, rushing into the room.

"Has the doctor arrived yet?"

"No, my lord."

"Have you ever delivered a baby?"

"No, my lord."

"Has anyone on the staff delivered a baby?"

"I don't know, my lord, but Cook has had eight babies. She no doubt knows a bit about birthing."

"Yes! Run down and send her up. Then come up and help her."

"Yes, my lord."

"This wasn't how I'd—oh!—planned the birth of our first—oh!—babe to be," Emma said.

"Me either, Em, but it will be something we'll never forget."

"Yes, it will," she replied, then cried out in pain.

Just then, the door opened and the Carnhaven cook entered the room. She was still tying on a clean, fresh apron.

"Hello, Cook." Emma greeted her the same as she would had the queen just walked in the room.

"Good afternoon, my lady. I take it your little one doesn't want to wait for the doctor to arrive?"

"No, I don't think he does."

Cook didn't even pause before she readied Emma to birth her child. The only time she stopped moving was when Emma had another pain. "Hold her hand, my lord. She needs someone to hold on to."

"Is that what you do when…you know…when it's you?" Emma asked.

"Oh, yes, my lady. I hold on to my husband's hand real tight so he can't get away. That way when the pains get too bad, he's close enough I can hit him real hard."

"Oh!" Emma cried out.

Spencer couldn't tell if her cry was one of pain or of laughter. He tried to be sympathetic, but he couldn't stop himself from laughing.

"Get ready, my lady. Your babe's almost ready to make an appearance."

"Already? I heard it sometimes takes days."

"And something only minutes."

"Oh."

Cook stepped to the head of the bed and gave Emma instructions on how to breathe, and what she wanted her to do when she ordered her to *push*.

"Very well, my lord. Now it's time for you to help out."

Spencer looked up in surprise. "I thought that's what I had been doing."

"Not quite. I need you to remove your jacket and roll up your shirt sleeves."

Spencer did as he was instructed. "Now what do you want me to do?"

"I want you to get ready to catch your baby when it's born."

"*What?*"

"You're going to be there to hold your child when it's born. Helen," Cook called out. "Get some blankets ready. Ruth," she called out to another upstairs maid. "Have a basin of water ready to wash our new arrival. I brought a knife to cut the cord, so that's taken care of."

Spencer watched everyone rush around the bed doing everything Cook demanded, then Emma interrupted everything with a long, loud cry as Cook lifted her almost to a sitting position.

"Get ready, Lord Carnhaven. Your babe wants to meet its father."

Spencer focused on the spot where his child should make an appearance and held out his hands to help his child enter the world.

Someone placed a warm blanket over his hands and arms, and he cradled the babe next to him. "It's a boy, Em! A boy!"

"Here," a male voice said close by. "Let me help you," he said, taking Spencer's son from him.

"Thank you, Dr. Edwards. I'm so glad you arrived."

"I was watching your team from the doorway, and I almost turned around and went home. Everyone looked as though they had everything under control."

"They did," Spencer said, then rushed to the head of the bed and clasped Emma's hands in his. "You gave us a son, Em. A son with a full head of hair the same color as mine."

"That's exactly what I prayed for. A strong, healthy baby boy who looked just like his father."

"Then your prayer was answered. That's what we got."

"What should we name him?" Emma asked.

"We will name him Andrew. And call him Drew."

"I like that," Emma said. "We'll name him Andrew Isaac Spencer, after his father and our friend."

"Yes," Spencer said, kissing his wife as she fell asleep.

JANEY CAME TO visit Emma every day, and the girls came to see her several times a day. They each took turns holding their brother and talking to him as if he were old enough to understand them.

Lady Cassandra read Jane Austen to him, and Felicity introduced him to Alexandre Dumas. And Emma read him *Tommy Turtle*.

"How is Andrew doing today?" Spencer asked when he came to check on her, which he did several times every day.

"He is a perfect baby," Emma answered.

"Of course he is. He comes from two perfect parents and two perfect sisters. How could he be anything else?"

Emma laughed. "How your tune will change when he throws his first tantrum."

Spencer reached out so his son could grasp his finger. "Tantrums will not be allowed, Master Drew. Just remember that so we don't have to reprimand you."

"Yes," Emma said. "We'll send you to bed with only bread and water."

"Don't worry, Lord Andrew. I'll sneak you up some cookies and milk."

"You would, wouldn't you, Spence?"

"Of course. That's what papas do." Spencer sat on the edge of the bed then leaned over Emma and kissed her. "Have I told you lately that I love you?"

"Yes, this morning before you left for breakfast."

"Oh, that was ages ago. You need to hear it again. I love you, Em. More than the sun, moon, and stars."

"And I love you." She cupped her palm to his cheek. "And I'd love you even more if you'd take me for a walk in the garden."

Spencer laughed. "Oh, I walked right into that, didn't I?"

"Yes, you did, but I really would enjoy a walk in the fresh air. And I'd like to take the girls with us."

"You would?"

"Yes, we need to spend more time with them. Andrew has been getting so much attention lately, I don't want them to feel slighted."

"Has anyone told you lately how wise you are?"

Emma handed the baby off to Helen, then reached up to kiss her husband. "No one needs to tell me that. I already know it."

"Oh," he said on a laugh. "I'm going to have to stop paying you so many compliments. Your head is beginning to swell."

Emma laughed as Spencer picked her up in his arms and carried her to the stairs. He carried her down and had one of the maids ask their daughters to join them in the library. When they reached the library, he had one of their outdoor servants follow them with a box he'd purchased in town.

"What is that?" Emma asked as they walked down the garden path.

"A surprise," he answered.

"For whom?"

"Not you, sweetheart. It's for another of my sweethearts."

Emma laughed. "Oh, I have competition," she said.

"No, not competition. You are beyond competition. Just another of my sweethearts."

"I see," she replied as they reached the gazebo in the center of the garden. Just then, the girls came up behind them.

"Where's Andrew?" Cassie asked, looking around.

"We didn't bring Andrew," Spencer answered. "This is an outing just for us. For me and my girls."

"Oh," the girls said excitedly.

"And what is that?" Felicity asked, pointing to the box that lay on the bench surrounding the gazebo.

"That is a present," Spencer answered. "Would either of you like a present?"

"What is it?" Cassie asked.

"It's a surprise," Spencer answered.

"I would like to know what it is before I say whether I'd like it or not."

"I see. What about you, Felicity?"

"I would like to have it, Papa."

"Before you even know what it is?"

"Yes, Papa."

"Very well. You may have it."

He motioned for the servant to give the present to Felicity. When she had it in her hands, she carefully unwrapped it, then opened the box.

"Oh, Papa," she said excitedly. "It's just what I wanted."

"What is it?" Cassie asked, looking into the box but not recognizing the present.

Felicity jumped up, ran to her father, and heartily hugged him. "Thank you, Papa. Thank you. But it's not my birthday."

"No, it's no one's birthday. It's just a special day."

"What is it?" Cassie repeated with a hint of frustration in her voice.

"It's a fishing rod," Emma answered her.

"A fishing rod?"

"Yes, Cassie," Spencer said. "Would you like to have your very own fishing rod?"

Cassie thought for a moment, then asked, "Would I have to touch a dead fish?"

"Of course you would, Cassie," Felicity answered.

"Then no. I don't want my own fishing rod."

Spencer reached into his pocket and took out two small blue velvet boxes. He handed one to each of his daughters.

"What is it, Papa?" Cassandra asked.

"Open it and see."

They both opened their boxes to find dainty diamond necklaces inside.

"Oh, they are beautiful!" both girls exclaimed.

"I'm glad you like them," Spencer said, then turned to Emma. "You'll find your gift in bed beneath your pillow," he said while the girls were putting on their necklaces.

"I find the only gift I need lying with his head on the pillow next to mine every morning."

Spencer leaned over and kissed his wife. He would enjoy days like this every day for the rest of his life.

In this life and the life beyond.

About the Author

Laura Landon taught high school for ten years before leaving the classroom to open her own ice-cream shop. As much as she loved serving up sundaes and malts from behind the counter, she closed up shop after penning her first novel. Now she spends nearly every waking minute writing, guiding her heroes and heroines to find their happily ever afters.

She is the author of more than a dozen historical novels, including SILENT REVENGE, INTIMATE DECEPTION, and her newest Montlake Romance release, INTIMATE SURRENDER.

Her books are enjoyed by readers around the world.

www.ingramcontent.com/pod-product-compliance
Lightning Source LLC
Chambersburg PA
CBHW070401200726
48294CB00003B/1036

* 9 7 8 1 9 6 1 2 7 5 6 3 8 *